2001

MW01710992

To

Debby

Happy Reading!

Don M. McKay

JOSEPHINE REMEMBERS

AND OTHER STORIES

DON M. MCKAY

BLACK HAT PUBLISHING

This book is a work of fiction. Names, characters, places, and incidents are either the product of the author's imagination or are used fictitiously. Any similarity to actual events, or persons, living or dead, is entirely coincidental.

Copyright © 2001 by Don M. McKay

Member	Writers Guild of Alberta
Member	Calgary Writers Association
Member	Book Publishers Association of Alberta

First Edition	May 2001

Author	Don M. McKay
Photo	(S. L. McKay) D. M. McKay
Cover Design	S. M. McKay

No part of this book may be reproduced or transmitted in any form by any means, electronic or mechanical, including photocopying, recording or any information storage, retrieval and transmission systems now known or to be invented, without permission in writing from Black Hat Publishing. This includes the right to reproduce this book or parts thereof in any form. The exception to the above is for the quotation of passages by a reviewer, in print or through the electronic mass media.

Canadian Cataloguing in Publication Data

McKay, Don M. (Don Malcolm), 1942-
Josephine remembers, and other stories
ISBN 0-9685331-1-6

1. Title.

PS8575.K282J687 2001 C813'.54 C2001-910605-X
PR9199.3.M3233J687 2001

This edition is published by Black Hat Publishing,
5208 44 Ave. NW, Calgary, Ab, T3A 0L8.

Printed and bound in Calgary, Alberta, Canada

ACKNOWLEDGEMENTS

I wish to extend my deepest appreciation and gratitude to my friends, colleagues and family members. Developing Josephine Remembers And Other Stories into a quality publication was made possible as a result of this special group of people freely giving of their time and talents.

DEDICATION

This book owes its very existence to the skills and advice of Barb, my most special wife. Her unlimited support and love have enabled me to persevere in the writing of the stories contained within this my second book.

Also, I dedicate this book to our daughter, Sheri, and our son, Scott, with my deepest thanks for patiently listening to their father as he regaled them with a myriad of story ideas.

INTRODUCTION

This collection of eight stories takes the reader on a journey through a variety of human experiences ranging from the deeply tragic to the comical. It is shown in the story *Josephine Remembers* that the love of family and friends can heal the effects of a tragic accident and reunite two special people. *Steel Friends* is initially set in the midst of World War II. The lives of two proud warriors' intertwine and as time passes, a very special friendship develops. In *The Arrows of Justice* Johnny suffers the death of his parents. Friends and family help him resolve his problems. *The Protector* provides amusement for the reader as the story follows the antics of a cat who attempts to protect her family from a mouse. In *The Black Tunnel* a policeman learns to respect the skills of his fellow officer. *The Kindred Spirit* shows us that sometimes there is more to our relationships with our friends than meets the eye. Romance is kindled in the hearts of two lonesome people through *The Chance Meeting* at an airport. Our lives are like *Pathways* that we travel on and when they intersect their directions can be changed forever.

I hope that *Josephine Remembers And Other Stories* gives you great pleasure as you begin your reading adventure.

Don M. McKay

TABLE OF CONTENTS

JOSEPHINE REMEMBERS

PART I

PROLOGUE

One day, a tragic accident occurred on the highway just past the small rural community of Anderson, Alberta. The sole survivor, Ron Latimer, severely traumatized by the accident, suffered a total memory loss.

On the same day, a small child and her Golden Labrador were found lying in a farmer's field. This mysterious incident completely baffled everyone. Eventually, Ruth and Frank Macdonald came forward to adopt little Josephine and her dog, Rosy. They gave Josephine a warm, loving home.

Some years later, a fortuitous event caused Josephine and Ron to come together by chance. Ron, whose memory was gradually returning, recognized Rosy, the Golden Labrador. Slowly, painfully, as his head throbbed, he realized that the girl who was singing to him was *his daughter!* A song that

Ron had once sung to Josephine struck a chord in *her* memory. Suddenly, Josephine realized that this was *her daddy!*

Later, Josephine had asked Ruth and Frank if Ron could come and live in their home because as she said, *"Mom…Ron, my father, doesn't have a home. I don't think he has anyone to love him. Do you think we could be his new family?"*

PART II

Ron stood staring out of the windows of the Anderson Care Centre thinking, *'I've been told about my accident by the police and Dr. Brown, but I don't really remember it. I wish I could remember more of my past. But…at least now I know I have a daughter! I am so lucky that Josephine is giving me the chance through her innocent, trusting love to come to know her. Ruth and Frank Macdonald have been devoted loving parents to her for seven years. They are in every real sense of the word, Josephine's parents.'*

In front of the windows were four plush chairs clustered around a small teakwood coffee table. Ron wandered over to one of chairs, sat down across from Dr. Brown and glanced upward. In the distance, he saw the two motionless figures sitting on the crest of the hill.

Ron's face had a puzzled expression as he spoke to his friend and psychiatrist."Do Josephine and Rosy go up the hill often?"

Dr. Brown ran his fingers through his graying beard and then slowly smoothed back his long hair.

"Yes, they do. Every Monday and Wednesday in the late afternoon, Ruth, Frank, and Josephine are here at the Care Centre singing and playing for the patients when I come to do my rounds. Josephine *is* a quiet eleven-year-old girl, but she has a special sparkling manner about her in how she uses her music to relate to the individual patients. The patients just love to sit with her and Rosy as she entertains. Between the broad musical training that Frank and Ruth have given that talented girl and her own natural abilities, she is really something to behold. Of course Rosy much to the distress and amusement of the nurses manages to introduce a bit of howling to the singing. After they are finished, Josephine and Rosy always go up the hill before they go home. On weekends as I have driven into town with my wife to see my parents, we have spotted Josephine up on the hill many times. Ruth and Frank tell me that she always takes Rosy for a walk up to the hill at least once a day. They told me they asked Josephine why she always goes up there, but she didn't know. She told them that sometimes she feels empty, as though she has lost something important, so she goes up there."

"But why now, since she's found me?"

"I don't know, Ron. Perhaps she still needs to go to the hill to fill some other emptiness, or to bring something to a resolution. Then again, it might simply be a place for her to be by herself with her thoughts."

"Today I'm going to begin my stay at the Macdonalds. It was wonderful that they invited me into their home. Ruth and Frank are Josephine's parents now and I have a hard time believing they would welcome me into their home and allow me the opportunity to get to know my daughter."

"Ron, I have watched Frank and Ruth work with their students at the school as well as the patients in this Care Centre. They are very special, kind, giving people. My opinion is that staying with the Macdonalds will certainly help spur on the recovery of your memory and will help you in forming a relationship with Josephine. However, to help your recovery along, we need to somehow re-enact your accident scene in a manner that will help break down your memory block of that incident."

"Gene, with all due respect I don't believe that it will do any good. Remember that we tried going out to the accident scene before, and all that experience gave me was a migraine headache. I'm just thankful that I found Josephine and Rosy. Anyway, Gene, I've been given the opportunity to have a visit with my daughter, so I don't intend to squander one precious moment. If I don't run into you before our next session, I'll see you this coming Wednesday."

"Goodbye, Ron. Good luck!"

Gene Brown watched as Ron, carrying a duffel bag slung over his shoulder, walked down the street toward the Macdonald's house. A smile crossed his face as he thought, '*Ron, I think that you will find in the coming days that your life will become a bit more complicated than a simple visit. Whether you like it or not, you are now part of the Macdonald's lives and a member of this town. You are my friend, therefore, I will do everything in my power to make sure you fully recover not only for you, but for Josephine.*'

Ron walked slowly down the front walk of the Macdonald's large rambling cedar sided house. Despite being excited at having the opportunity to come to know his daughter, he was extremely concerned that he not allow himself to interfere in the Macdonald's family life.

As Ron reached to ring the doorbell, a booming voice rang out, "Hey, Ron, come on up here to the front deck. Ruth and I are just enjoying the fine taste of a new drink that I concocted in the kitchen. You have to try this creation made from freshly squeezed fruit juices, ice cream, and ginger ale and give me your opinion."

Shielding his eyes from the sun, Ron stared up toward the deck where he could see Ruth and Frank with drinks in their hands. Walking up onto the deck, he sat down in a lawn chair across from them. Ruth picked up Ron's duffel bag and went inside the house. She returned in a few minutes with a tall glass of Frank's creation for him.

"Ron, I've put your bag in our back bedroom. You'll find that it has its own large bathroom." She grinned at Frank. "In fact, Ron, you'll see that everything in our home is large and spacious. After all, it was built by my big talented husband and his friends." She winked at Frank who grinned back at her.

"I don't know how to thank the two of you for giving me this chance to be with you and Josephine. I'll make my visit short so that I don't interfere unduly with your lives."

Frank and Ruth gazed at each other for a few minutes. Leaning toward Ron, Frank's voice took on a serious tone.

"Ron, you are welcome in our home. Time restrictions on how long you are here do not exist. See that young lady coming down the hill? Well, she has filled our lives with love and happiness. Josephine has asked that we accept you into our family, therefore so far as Ruth and I are concerned, you are now a part of us."

At that moment Josephine, her hair flying behind her, came bounding up the stairs of the deck followed immediately by Rosy. She skipped over to Ruth and Frank and gave them each a hug. Turning toward Ron, Josephine stepped forward.

"Hello! Is it okay if I give you a welcoming hug?"

Ron looked at Ruth and Frank who just simply sat and smiled.

"Yes, Josephine. A hug would really be nice."

Josephine leaned over Ron while he wrapped his arms around her. He found himself drawing close to tears as he sat there with his daughter in his arms after so many years. Josephine released her hold on Ron, then walked over to sit on a lawn chair. Staring intently into Ron's eyes, she started to talk.

"When Rosy and I were up on the hill, we got to wondering about a few things. I know that Dr. Brown said that my first mom was killed in the accident, but I found you, so maybe my mom wasn't killed and maybe I'll find her too."

Ron shook his head. "Josephine, Dr. Brown told me that there is no question—your mother was killed in the accident."

"Can you tell me about my mom?"

"I can't, Josephine. I'm sorry. I just remember a few bits and pieces of my life. I don't even remember the accident."

Josephine removed her locket from around her neck. Twisting the back of the locket in a counter-clockwise motion, she opened it. Then she studied the picture of herself, Ron, and a lady.

"But this picture in my locket...isn't this lady my mom?"

"Yes, I think she must be, Josephine. You and I are with her."

* * *

In the next couple of weeks after Ron had moved in with the Macdonalds, Josephine carefully avoided calling him by any name, until one evening she appeared in the front room where Ron was sitting by himself. She wandered over to the grand piano where she practiced some music for the

Rotarian Family Night. Finally, she sat down on the floor and crossed her long legs. With an intense look on her face, she peered up at him, her sandy brown eyebrows furled into a frown, her green eyes studying him.

Ron smiled and gently asked, "Josephine, you look troubled. Is there something wrong?"

Josephine leaned over, looking at her hands. She smoothed back an errant strand of hair, then shyly looked back up at Ron.

She mumbled, "I don't know what to call you."

"Oh, Josephine, you may call me whatever name makes you the most comfortable. I remember that some of the guys at university used to call me R. W. because my middle name is William. You could call me that. Or else Ron or Uncle Ron would be fine.

"You are my father, not my uncle, and I feel a little awkward calling a grown-up by his first name."

"Josephine, why don't you think about it and then make a decision."

Josephine slowly rose and went to sit at the piano. She quietly sang, *The Tennessee Waltz,* as she glanced at Ron out of the corners of her eyes, and then gazed out of the front room window. Her voice swelled in volume as her full lips widened into a large grin. After she had completed the lovely old song, she got up and wandered out to the kitchen. Silently sneaking over to the cookie jar, she eased open the lid and took out a soft molasses gingerbread cookie. Sitting down at the table, she watched Ruth scurrying around the kitchen making final preparations to a baking dish full of Lasagna. Ruth finished her job, looked out of the kitchen window, and then studied Josephine out of the corners of her deep brown eyes. Then, she quietly walked over to her. She grinned as she leaned over and kissed Josephine on the forehead.

"Josephine, is that a cookie I see filling your mouth? You seem kind of down. J. J., what seems to be the trouble?"

"Nothing, just thinking. Everything is okay."

Ruth went to the cupboard, took out two glasses, filled them with milk and placed them on the table. Then sat down next to Josephine. She placed a hand over her precious daughter's, and looked at her with a gentle smile. It was quiet in the kitchen, only the birds could be heard outside the window as they noisily squawked while they fed at the bird feeder. Ruth waited patiently for Josephine.

Finally, Josephine turned slowly to face Ruth, "Mom, do you think that dad would be mad if I called Ron, Daddy Ron?"

"I think your dad would be okay with that, Josephine."

"I really love dad. Kids at school say that dad is a tough, no-nonsense, fair teacher and if they need help, he is the man to see. When Curtis Bromley's parents broke up, he really started to misbehave. Dad encouraged him to become a member of the band. Everyday they practiced their electronic keyboards and after that, they'd have a chat. Dad is always doing things like that for Kelly and me. Mom, I don't want to hurt his feelings. It's just that…well, Ron is my dad too and I just think he needs a special name."

Tears pooled in Josephine's eyes, then ran down her cheeks. Ruth gave Josephine a tissue, then wrapped her arms around this special daughter who had, in her own quiet way, given Ruth so much joy.

Ruth whispered, "J. J., it's okay. I'm positive your dad will be fine with you calling Ron, Daddy Ron."

"Mom, would you go outside and tell dad what we've decided?"

"No, Josephine. You're almost twelve and a young lady, and I think you should tell your dad yourself when he comes in from the garage. Here's another tissue. Now, dry your tears. Don't worry, I'll sit right here with you. Okay?"

"Okay."

At that moment, the screen door slammed and Frank's large frame filled the back entrance as he came stomping into the kitchen. He appeared to be completely covered with dust from working in the garage. Josephine's eyes immediately shifted downward as she focussed on her hands. Ruth walked up to Frank at the sink, hugged him from behind and reached up to kiss him tenderly on the ear. She whispered something, then left and went back to sit at the table beside Josephine. Frank glanced at Josephine, winked at Ruth and then started to wash his face and hands. When he had finished cleaning up, he walked over to Josephine to give her a hug.

Josephine's voice was a tremulous whisper as she blurted out, "Daddy Ron—I'm going to call him Daddy Ron." Her eyes nervously stared upward at Frank waiting for his reaction.

Frank grinned as he leaned over to give Josephine another hug.

"Daddy Ron is a great name, J. J. I'm glad you finally found a name for Ron. Have you told him yet?"

"No, Dad. I wanted to make sure that it was okay with you, first."

Frank smiled, "I think it's perfect, Josephine."

"J. J., you had better go and tell Ron. Supper will be ready soon," added Ruth.

Rising out of her chair, Josephine reached up as Frank bent over and she gave him a big kiss. "Thank you, Dad!"

"It's okay, J. J.! Now, you'd better do as mom says and tell Ron what you've decided."

Ruth and Frank grinned as they watched Josephine walk into the front room and slowly sit on the couch beside Ron. They stood peeking into the front room, Frank with his arm around Ruth's waist, and listened while Josephine spoke to Ron in a very serious grown-up voice.

"I have decided that your name will be Daddy Ron because you are my daddy and your name is Ron. Okay?" she asked.

"That would be great, Josephine! I think that a big hug is in order!"

Josephine's eyes darted sideways toward the kitchen door. Ruth and Frank both nodded their heads.

"I think it would be all right."

As Ron hugged Josephine, he used his left hand to quickly wipe away the tears that had formed in his eyes. Just then the bell on the oven rang indicating that the Lasagna was ready for supper, and Ruth and Frank entered the room.

Ruth smiled broadly at Josephine, and then she looked at Frank and Ron.

"All right, guys, it's suppertime."

As Ron started to walk into the kitchen, he took out a tissue and wiped his eyes again. Frank glanced down at Ron as he walked beside him, then reached down to put his arm around Ron's shoulder.

Ruth smiled at Josephine as she whispered, "Josephine, I'm very proud of you, that was very kind."

Josephine wiped her eyes, then gave a little smile.

As she sat down at the table, she announced, "Mom, I'm really hungry."

Rosy laid down on the floor beside her chair.

The next day, Ron went to see Dr. Brown at the Care Centre. He walked over to the waiting room's huge windows and stood looking up at the hill.

Dr. Brown watched him for a little while, then spoke. “Ron, what are you thinking about?”

“Gene, I would like you to bring me my trunk that has my stuff in it from Calgary.”

“I’ll be glad to bring your trunk here for you. I remember you told me that none of the things in it meant anything to you, but it’s been five years since we looked at your things.”

“Fragments of my memory seem to be slowly returning either in dreams or during the day when I’m walking around town. I think that if I could have the trunk, it might hurry up the process.”

“Okay. The next time I come up from Calgary, I’ll bring it. Have you reconsidered your position about going back out to the accident scene? I still think that we need to try again to break that blockage.”

“No, Gene, it wouldn’t do any good. Please don’t bring it up again.”

* * *

One evening while Ruth, Frank, Josephine, and Ron were eating supper, a knock came at the back door. A man with a grey, handlebar moustache, glittering dark eyes, and wearing a black Stetson peered in through the back screen door.

Frank laughed as he called out, “Hey, Ross, come on in and have some dinner.”

Ross Reynolds, a big, rawboned, muscular

man, strode into the kitchen. He grabbed a chair, pulled it up to the table, turned it around backwards and sat down.

Ruth said, "Josephine, would you get Ross some stew, please?" Ruth went over to the coffeepot, poured Ross a cup, then filled a plate with some fresh gingersnap cookies.

"Ross, it's great to see you, but I thought you were up to your eyeballs with your crops and cattle," stated Frank.

Ross threw his Stetson under his chair and ate a couple of hefty forkfuls of stew before he replied, "You're ruddy right, I'm busy. In fact, that's the whole problem—we are too darn busy! Frank, I was wondering if you could drive combine for me in the evenings from seven to nine o'clock for a couple of weeks? My hired man and I need to do some work with the cattle."

Staring thoughtfully at the ceiling, Frank leaned way back on his chair.

Turning to Ross he said, "Ross, I've got a great idea." He grinned as he looked over at Ruth, Josephine, and Ron and continued to speak. "Ruth used to drive truck for her dad out on their farm when she was growing up and I'm sure we can show Ron how to handle your second truck. Josephine and Rosy could ride in the trucks as swampers. If everyone is agreeable, then the Macdonald crew could handle things from five until nine for the next two weeks. How would that be?"

Ruth and Ron smiled, then nodded in agreement.

Josephine exclaimed, "It sounds like fun, Dad. May Kelly come too?"

"Okay, but only if she gets her parents' permission."

The first couple of evenings at the Reynolds's spread went without incident, but on the third evening, a momentous event happened to Ron and to Josephine.

It was almost nine o'clock when the clouds that had completely obscured the mountains from view began rolling down the valleys of the foothills and advancing steadily toward the Reynolds's spread.

Ron had just unloaded his truck at the Alberta Wheat Pool Elevator in Anderson when Ruth's voice suddenly sounded on his radio.

"Ron, I'm just coming in with a load. Frank wants you to 'put the pedal to the metal', and get out there quickly. He says that we are rapidly losing visibility with these low-lying clouds, but if you can make one more run, we'll be finished that section. Then tomorrow we can start working on Ross's final field."

"Okay, Ruth! But it will still take me about twenty minutes to get out there."

"Ron, take Highway 22 south out of town. Two kilometres beyond the outskirts, you'll find an access road to the Reynolds's land. You can drive right through the north field—it'll be a little shorter."

Josephine and Kelly sitting in the cab of the truck watched as Ron's hands started to shake.

Beads of sweat slowly formed on his forehead. Josephine placed her hands gently on Ron's arm.

"Daddy Ron, are you okay?"

Kelly spoke up, "What's the problem, Mr. L.?"

Ron slowly picked up the radio's microphone, "Ruth, I don't know if I can go that way. It's where the accident took place."

Josephine and Kelly stared with round, wide eyes and open mouths.

"Ron, you told us that you went out there with Gene Brown, but you didn't remember anything. So there's nothing to be afraid of—is there?"

"No… I guess not."

Ron drove rapidly out to the access road. He entered Reynolds's fields, driving slowly along the dirt track until he saw the lights of the huge combine. Turning the truck, he lined it up with the combine, then he waved at Frank when he had the box of the truck under the combine's hopper. Frank emptied the wheat from the combine into the truck. Then he shut down the combine and got into the truck with Josephine, Kelly, Ron, and Rosy.

By this time the clouds had touched the ground, thus restricting visibility to a couple of hundred metres. Ron with Frank's guidance drove along the dirt track until he approached the access road into the field. Just as he began to cross the ditch where the access road joined Highway 22, two sets of lights shone on the grain truck and air horns blasted. Bringing the truck to a lurching stop, Ron bolted out of the cab and disappeared into the dense fog as he ran off down the road toward town. Josephine and Rosy peeled out of the truck running in the opposite direction. Frank and Kelly jumped quickly from the truck and began to run after Josephine. They found her and Rosy sitting in front of the combine, looking up at the huge machine.

Ruth drove up, then quickly ran to join the others.

Frank wrapped his arms around Josephine who looked up at him and said, "Where's my mommy and daddy?"

"Ron decided to walk into town, Josephine," Frank quietly said.

Josephine looked deeply into Frank's eyes. Several moments passed.

"Dad, I don't know why I said that. I don't even know why I ran back here."

"It's okay, Josephine."

Ruth knelt in front of Josephine. "Are you okay, J. J.?"

"I'm fine, Mom. Can we go and look for Daddy Ron? It's not good that he's out there all alone."

"Josephine, we'll try to find Ron on our way into town, but we have to drop off the grain and Kelly. Her parents will start worrying if we don't get her back on time. Are you sure you're all right?"

"Yes, Mom."

On their journey into town Frank, Ruth, Kelly, and Josephine watched for Ron, but never did see him. Later on, however, they found Ron at home quietly sitting in the front room before a roariing fire.

Ron simply said, "I'm sorry, folks. I guess I got spooked out there with the fog and air horns. It won't happen again."

Josephine ran over to Ron and gave him a big hug.

Ruth smiled. "Are you okay, Ron?"

"Yes, I think so. I'm very tired, folks. My head is splitting—I think I'm developing a migraine headache. I'm going to go to bed now."

Later that evening, Frank and Ruth quietly stole out of the house. They met Bill, Ross, and Gene down at the local restaurant. The three men sat in a booth eating huge pieces of apple pie with ice cream and sipping large mugs of steaming hot coffee. The moment that Ross saw Frank and Ruth, he yelled at the waitress to bring more pie and coffee.

Gene looked expectantly at the Macdonalds.

"Well, folks, do you think it worked?"

Frank and Ruth both shrugged their shoulders.

Ruth mumbled, "I don't know, Gene. Ron never gave any indication that he remembered anything. Josephine seems like she's inside herself, trying to figure things out. Thanks Bill and Ross for driving the trucks and trying to help us."

Both men nodded their heads.

Gene Brown leaned back thoughtfully, contemplating the ceiling. "You know, the memory is a funny thing. Sometimes even though a blockage is broken, memory can return very slowly or sporadically. It depends on the individual person. Let's not give up yet."

Two days later, Ron went to his next session with Gene Brown. Gene had brought Ron's trunk in his van. After the session, Ron and Dr. Brown took the trunk to the Macdonald's house. Big brawny Frank helped the other two men load the trunk into Ron's bedroom. In the coming days while Ruth, Frank, and Ron helped Ross with the combining, the trunk stayed in Ron's bedroom unopened, but during the evenings, Ron would go to his bedroom and spend hours looking inside it. As Ruth, Frank, and Josephine began to get more involved at school, Ron began fixing suppers for them. He spent his days going for long walks and thinking about the items in his trunk.

The first evidence that the staging of the accident had jarred Ron's memory was during one therapeutic session when he suddenly blurted out, "I remember the fog and the noise and the lights and then everything went black!"

During the next few sessions, Ron indicated that his memories were now rapidly returning. He said that his past memories before the accident were now like a torrent of water flooding into his brain, unfortunately, they were also like shards of a broken mirror being fused back together in a helter-skelter pattern.

* * *

Having two dads caused some interesting

situations for Josephine, Ron, and the Macdonalds. One Friday, Josephine's grade seven homeroom class came noisily bounding into their room at the end of the school day. They had just returned from a very active period of aerobics. Sonia Melnyk, a pretty, young first year teacher, taught the class Mathematics and was their homeroom supervisor. Josephine and Kelly sat down in their desks across from each other. They giggled and grinned at one another as they covertly admired Sonia's latest hairdo, her makeup, and her brightly coloured print dress. On each desk, Sonia had placed an envelope with the student's parents' names written on it.

Josephine looked at the names on her envelope, then slowly shook her head. Sonia, assuming her best teacher posture at the front of the class, started to speak.

"All right, class, let's settle down. Your homework for the weekend is on the board." Several good-natured groans echoed throughout the class. "Please make sure you have copied it into your assignment books. On your desks are tickets for you and your parents for the annual Anderson Rotarian Family Banquet which, as you know, will be held at the arena next Friday. Josephine, you have a question?"

"Miss Melnyk, my envelope just says Ruth and Frank Macdonald. I need one more ticket."

"I'm sorry, Josephine, but everyone has been given two tickets for their parents and that's all we have."

"But I have two dads, Miss Melnyk!"

Josephine wailed.

A couple of boys laughed and one of them blurted out, "Come on, Miss Melnyk. We know you're new, but didn't you know that Josephine has two dads?"

"No, I didn't know!"

Kelly jumped out of her desk, her fist clenched, and began advancing menacingly toward the two boys who pretended to cower in abject horror.

"Sit down, Kelly," commanded Sonia. She gave the boys a withering glance. They quickly straightened in their desks and adopted looks of pure innocence.

Josephine looked down at her desk, her face red.

She mumbled, "I won't hurt Daddy Ron's feelings. My whole family has to go to the banquet to hear Kelly and me sing, or I'm not going."

"I'm not going either if Mr. L. doesn't get to go," piped up Kelly.

Sonia dismissed the class when the bell rang and asked the two girls to stay behind. She walked slowly down the aisle to sit on a student's desk in front of the girls.

"I don't understand, Josephine. Who is your other dad?"

"He's my Daddy Ron. I lost him when I was four-years-old, but now he's come back."

"You mean he left you and your mother all alone?"

"No. He had a terrible accident up near the

Reynolds's ranch. Daddy Ron spent a long time in the hospital and couldn't remember me. My mom died."

"Oh, Josephine. I'm so sorry. Where is your Daddy Ron living?"

"In my house with Rosy and me and, of course, my mom and dad."

Sonia Melnyk was sitting staring at Josephine and trying to understand what she was hearing when a deep voice interrupted her thoughts.

"Sonia...Josephine, Ruth, and I insisted that Ron live with us," said Frank. He stood in the doorway of the classroom. "After all, as Josephine has said, Daddy Ron has no one to love and we are his new family."

Sonia smiled as she watched Ruth and Frank walk into the room.

"Frank and Ruth, that is one of nicest stories that I have heard in a long time, but we do have a bit of a problem. I don't have any more tickets for the banquet. As you know, Mayor Fulbrook brings them to the school on behalf of the Rotarians."

Josephine looked thoughtfully out of the window of the classroom.

"Kelly and I could go over to the Fulbrook's house and get another ticket."

Sonia laughed, "I think Josephine has just found the solution."

Ruth said to Josephine, "Go right over to the Fulbrook's house now, Josephine, and let the Mayor know that we need another ticket. Your dad and I will meet you at home."

Josephine and Kelly ran over to the Fulbrook's house, but were told by his wife that he was on an extended business trip in Calgary, and wouldn't be home until just an hour or so before the banquet.

When Josephine arrived home, she found Ruth and Frank giving Ron a hand with supper. Frank smiled at her as she walked in.

"So, Josephine, was there any problem getting Ron a ticket?"

"Just a little one, Dad, but it's going to be okay. Mayor Fulbrook is out of town, but he'll be back an hour before the concert and he'll make sure I get another one."

Josephine, her back to Frank, stealthily helped herself to a cookie from the jar on the counter.

Ruth shook her head as she spoke in a scolding tone, "J. J., you're going to spoil your supper."

"Mom, can't I just have one? You made my favourite soft gingerbread cookies and they are the best! I'm really hungry."

Ruth shook her head as she grinned at Josephine.

"Well, okay, that bit of flattery will get you one cookie, but just one."

Ron paused from peeling the potatoes and added, "Josephine, please don't worry about the ticket. It's probably kind of awkward showing up at the banquet with two dads. As I said when we found each other, I'd love it if we can be friends, but Frank is your dad. You folks go ahead. Don't worry about me."

Josephine quickly wheeled around and smiled at Ron.

"Daddy Ron, I already have your ticket."

She ran into the hall, then took the three tickets out of her book bag. Returning to the kitchen, she handed them to the two men and Ruth.

"I'll get my ticket later from Mayor Fulbrook. Kelly and I have been asked to sing a bunch of western songs. Well, actually, Kelly as usual opened her big mouth to volunteer us when the principal said the Rotarians would like a few school kids to provide some entertainment at the banquet. Dad and Mom, you probably know about it anyway seeing as you are our music teachers. Well, you know, I *am* Kelly's friend, so I guess we're singing. Mom, could you, dad, and Daddy Ron accompany us? I just wish the town had decided to install the new sound system in the arena this year rather than deciding to wait until next year."

"Sure, Josephine, we would all be glad to help. You're right, we do know about the entertainment. The principal told us all about it at the noon staff meeting. So far as the sound system is concerned, it's just that the town can't afford it right now, Josephine. We'll get by with the school's speakers and microphones."

Grinning, Ruth walked over to Josephine and kissed her on the forehead. She smoothed back Josephine's long sandy hair.

Turning back to face Ron and Frank, Ruth

said, "Well, guys, it's settled. You are both going to the banquet!"

Frank looked with deep amusement at Ron who stood at the sink looking across the backyard, obviously deep in thought. He was continuing to peel the potato that he had been working on, but it was quickly disappearing into the sink.

"Hey, Ron, you'd better take it easy on that potato or the next thing you peel will be your fingers!"

Ron's head jerked around so that he could look at Frank.

"Frank, do you think I could get a key to the arena?"

"I guess so, Ron, but why?"

"I thought I would set up a small stage for the girls with lights, speakers, and some microphones."

"Ron, are you sure that you can do that? I mean you would need to install some electric plugs, microphone connections, and a bunch of other stuff, wouldn't you? Besides, the town doesn't have money in the budget for that kind of renovation until next year."

"Frank...you, Ruth, and this town have been great to Josephine and me. For some reason electronics and electrical projects are things that really interest me. I seem to recall that I used to have a lot to do with things that dealt in those areas. I would love to see if I could set up something nice for the girls to use for their presentation next week."

"Okay, Ron. I'll phone the town hall in the morning and get us a key."

*   *   *

A week from Saturday, Josephine ran over to see Mayor Fulbrook. Mrs. Fulbrook told her that he had not yet returned, but as soon he did, they would come over to meet her at the entrance to the arena around five o'clock. Besides, they wouldn't miss the opportunity of visiting the families and of course, as Mayor of Anderson, he was expected to speak at the banquet.

Later that morning, Frank, Ron, and Ruth played their instruments for Kelly and Josephine as the girls practiced their songs in one final warm-up. After that, the men left packing their instruments under their arms and walking together over to the arena. Josephine and Kelly stayed at the Macdonald's house where they changed into jeans and matching western blouses. Ruth arranged Josephine's sandy hair and then Kelly's reddish auburn hair into identical hairdos. Then she stood back to admire her creations. She felt a strange mixture of emotions as she noticed how grown-up Josephine now appeared, and she thought to herself, '*My little girl is a beautiful young lady.*' Ruth collected her music from the grand piano and they all walked over to the arena together.

When Ruth, Josephine, and Kelly entered the arena, they saw Bill Sharpe dressed in a suit just inside the door, taking tickets from the parents and their children. It was obvious from the way he tugged at the neck of his dress shirt that he wished he could be in his old, faded, comfortable overalls that he wore at the service station. Kelly gave her ticket to Bill, spotted her parents and ran inside to say hello.

Josephine walked over to the large windows in the foyer and stood looking out. Ruth watched her for a few moments, then walked over to her.

"What's the matter, Josephine?"

"He didn't come to the arena. I wish people would keep their promises."

"Mayor Fulbrook?"

"Yes. Mrs. Fulbrook said the moment her husband came back from Calgary, they would come over and give me a ticket."

"I'm sure that something unforeseen must have happened, J. J."

"Now I can't go to the banquet! Kelly and I can't sing! I chose some of those songs as a surprise for Daddy Ron."

"J. J., that was very kind of you. Come on. Let's go talk to Bill about your problem."

"Mom, Mr. Sharpe can't do anything if I don't have a ticket. I'd just get him in trouble with the Rotarians. I'll just go home."

"Josephine, I want you to settle down. Now, come with me so that you can explain the problem to Bill."

Josephine, with a bit of encouragement from Ruth, explained the situation to Bill Sharpe who, much to her surprise, started to laugh.

"Josephine, you have been saying hello to me and sitting on the hill behind the station for seven years. We're pals, aren't we? Besides, you are part of the entertainment and that makes you one of our guests of honour. Wait until you see what Ron has whipped up for your and Kelly's performance!"

Josephine and Ruth entered the arena, then stopped and gasped in amazement. A low stage had been constructed with four microphones across the front edge. Spotlights hung down from the rafters and four huge professional speakers were spaced across the stage.

Josephine walked over to Ron.

"Wow! How did you create this beautiful setup for Kelly and me?"

"Well, I remembered some contacts that I used to know years ago and I made some phone calls."

"It's fantastic! Thank you, Daddy Ron."

Just then the Master of Ceremonies asked the students and their parents to go to their tables. The proceedings then began in a fine style with Josephine and Kelly singing a sterling rendition of the national anthem. Later, they entertained the audience with a medley of western songs. The program was brought to a close when Josephine, who was carrying a hand microphone, walked across the stage to stand beside Ron. She placed her right hand on Ron's shoulder and as Ron played the banjo, sang, *Mountain Dew* and *You Are My Sunshine.*

*　　*　　*

A week after the Anderson Town's Rotarian Family Night, Josephine was returning from her quarter horse riding practice when she heard music coming from her house. Quickly she waved goodbye to Kelly and ran up the front steps. Music flowed through the house as she was treated to the sight of Ron, Frank, and Ruth having an impromptu music session. Ruth was seated at the grand piano, Ron was playing the banjo and Frank was strumming on a guitar. When they spotted Josephine, they started to sing, *Mountain Dew*. Josephine ran over to the grand piano and sat down beside Ruth. She immediately joined the others and they finished the song together. Then, Ron's baritone voice started to sing, *Brahms' Lullaby*. Ruth and Frank glanced at each other as they played quietly in the background. Josephine hummed along as she listened to Ron.

When he was finished, Josephine grinned. "I know that tune. Would you teach me the words?"

Ron told Josephine the words to the lovely old ballad and she sang it a few times. After that, they sang it in unison in a delicate beautiful style. When Ron and Josephine finished the song, Ron hung his head and wiped his eyes. Josephine looked fondly up at Ruth.

"Mom...you used to sing that song to me when I was a little girl."

Ruth and Frank looked at each other with

puzzled frowns on their faces. Then Ruth smiled and put her arms around Josephine.

"No, J. J., I didn't, but it's a beautiful ballad. You and Ron sang it in a style that gives it a special beauty and charm."

"Mom, I'm sure you must have sung it to me when I was small. I know I've heard that tune before."

Ron stood and walked slowly over to the big bay window. He stared toward the hill, then, his voice choked with emotion, he hesitantly said, "Your mom...my wife... Sandra...sang *Brahms' Lullaby* to you every night when she tucked you into bed. It was the last song that she sang to you when she laid you down for a rest in the motorhome."

Slowly Josephine rose from the piano bench and walked over to Ron. She held out her hands to him as they looked into each other's eyes.

Then Ron quietly said, "Wait, Josephine. I'll be right back."

Ron turned and left the room. A few minutes later, he returned carrying with him a large coloured picture of a woman who had green eyes and sandy hair. The woman looked remarkably like Josephine.

Ron's voice was very quiet and filled with reverence as he spoke in a halting fashion, "Josephine...I want you...to have this picture...if it's all right with you, Ruth and Frank."

Ron looked over Josephine's head at Ruth and Frank who both nodded.

"It's my mom...isn't it?" Josephine asked in a quivering voice. "I know it is She looks just like me," she continued with awe in her voice.

"Yes, it's my wife, Sandra, and your first mom, Josephine. She loved you very much. I know that she would be so very proud that you have grown up to be such a beautiful fine young lady."

Ruth and Frank leaned over Josephine to look at the picture. Tears cascaded down Josephine's cheeks as she clutched the picture to her chest and fell to her knees.

Ruth knelt beside Josephine and whispered, "Please show me, J. J." Josephine tilted the picture forward and Ruth looked at it. Then she looked back at Josephine's face. "She is absolutely beautiful Josephine. She looks just like you."

Josephine slowly looked into Ron's eyes.

"Now can you tell me about my mom?"

"Yes, Josephine. My memory, thanks to the fellows forcing me to relive the accident, has started to return."

"Daddy Ron, how did the accident happen?"

"Didn't anyone tell you about it?"

"Well, Dr. Brown told us about the accident near Mr. Reynolds's place...and I know my mom was killed...but, I don't understand why our motorhome was on the Reynolds's access road."

Ron looked over toward Ruth and Frank.

Then he said, "Frank, will you tell your part of the story first?"

Frank sat back down on his chair and

looked into Ruth's eyes.

Her eyes looked back into Frank's, and then he mumbled, "Josephine, you remember that we told you that Ross and I found you in the Reynolds's wheat field when you were just a tiny little girl.

"Yes, Dad," Josephine answered.

Frank then looked over at Ron, as he continued the story.

"That morning Ross was combining his field and it was fortunate that Rosy managed to get his attention. Ross quickly stopped the combine. Nearby we found a beautiful little girl who was about four-years-old with long sandy hair. She kept telling us that she wanted her mommy and daddy. Back then we didn't know the little girl had any connection with the accident down the highway."

Josephine looked slowly from one adult to the other. Finally, she stood up, reached out and took one of Ron's hands.

"Why were we outside of Anderson? Please, Daddy Ron, I want to know."

Ron looked down at Josephine. Then he slowly continued the story.

"The fog was very thick that morning. I was turning the motorhome around, Josephine, and I never saw the two semi-trailer trucks."

"But why were you turning around?"

"I was going back to Bill's Service Station."

"Why?"

"Your mom and I were going to look for you."

"I don't understand. Where was I?"

"A few kilometres back while I was busy filling up, your mom popped into the store for a few minutes. You and Rosy were sleeping in the back of the motorhome. Josephine, you were a very little girl and somehow you must have slipped out of an open door when no one was looking and wandered off. Maybe you were looking for your mom. Rosy must have tagged along after you. Anyway, we had only gone a little way when your mom went back to check on you and that's when she discovered you and Rosy were missing. Of course, we were in a panic and immediately started back to find you."

Josephine took her hand out of Ron's, and fell to her knees. She grasped the picture with both hands and bent her head as tears rolled down her cheeks. Suddenly, Josephine's head tilted back as she looked at Ron with a look of horror.

She screamed, "No!" "I killed my mom! My mom loved me and I killed her!"

Ron quickly knelt down in front of Josephine. He wrapped his arms around her. "No, Josephine, if I hadn't had the accident your mom would be alive. It's my fault. You mustn't blame yourself for something that happened when you were only four-years- old. It's my fault that your mom died!"

Josephine stood and stepped back out of Ron's arms. Ruth and Frank came up behind her and put their hands gently on her shoulders. Just then, Rosy walked up in front of Josephine, sat and held out her paw. The Golden Labrador stared up into Josephine's tear-filled eyes. Josephine took Rosy's paw in her hand as she leaned over to lovingly nuzzle her friend who had been with her for all these years. She looked around the room at Ron, Ruth, and Frank. Then she vigorously shook her head.

"If I hadn't left, my mommy wouldn't have been killed and Daddy Ron wouldn't have been hurt! It's all my fault!"

Josephine suddenly bolted out of the room. The front screen door banged behind her as she leaped off the front steps and ran down the side-walk. Rosy tore by the adults as she raced after Josephine who had fled down the street. Frank, Ruth, and Ron, as one, ran to the door, but they were too late to catch the athletic eleven-year-old. Just then, a blue Yukon appeared on the street and drove into their driveway. Dr. Brown slowly got out as he looked questioningly at the group stand-ing on the front steps and then turned to gaze at the figure racing off into the distance.

Ruth looked at Dr. Brown with a look of deep concern. She told him what had happened between Josephine and Ron. Ron stood with his head bowed, looking at the ground. Dr. Brown, surprisingly, simply walked by the others and into the house. When Ron, Ruth, and Frank followed a few moments later, they found him sitting in the front room. He was quietly strumming on Frank's old acoustic guitar.

He looked up at Ruth and said, "Ruth, do you have any coffee and some of those famous homemade gingersnap cookies? I've had patients all morning and haven't had a chance to eat."

Ruth's shocked brown eyes flashed in anger as she said, "I don't understand why you're sitting there calmly asking for cookies while Josephine is terribly upset and has run away!"

"Ruth, we know where she's gone. She'll have raced up to the brow of the big hill—we know that's her favourite thinking place. Josephine needs time to herself to think and to grieve. Ruth, Rosy is with her and will take of her. Let's give her a bit of time to sort things out. Now as I said, I really am hungry."

"I'm sorry. I guess you're right, Gene. However, I don't think cookies are a good way to fill up that space. I'll fix you some lunch."

After Ruth had brought a tray of food to Dr. Brown, she quietly walked out of the room leaving the men by themselves.

Ron sat, elbows on his knees and head resting in his hands and gazed blankly off into space.

Frank sat motionless on the bench seat of their grand piano. It was obvious that their eleven-year daughter had determined that she was the cause of her mother's death. One could only guess at the emotions swirling around in Josephine's mind. Frank stood noiselessly, then walked across the floor to the front door to look through the screen. Ruth sat by herself in a lawn chair, gazing up toward Josephine and Rosy. Frank moved up quietly behind Ruth, slipping his arms around her shoulders. He took a tissue from his pocket to wipe the tears that coursed down her freckled cheeks.

"How are you doing?" Frank whispered softly.

"I'm okay, I guess. Frank, I'm worried about our daughter—I want to go to her. I want to hold her in my arms and make her hurt go away, but something tells me to hold back.

Ruth stood, turned and buried her head in Frank's chest. He wrapped his arms around her back. Ruth's body trembled and the muffled sounds of her crying could be heard. Frank stared over her head toward the hill where he could see the figures of Josephine and Rosy standing.

Picking his words carefully, he said, "Ruth, there are times when we all need to be by ourselves. Josie has Rosy up there with her. You know, I really believe Rosy will provide the emotional strength for Josephine to deal with this situation. Sweetheart, I think our role is to be here when Josephine comes back. We have to be strong and we have to continue to provide the most loving, happy environment we can for Josephine and Ron, so that things can just work themselves out."

Ruth dried her tears and gave Frank a big hug. Then she started to walk quickly toward the house.

"Where are you going?"

"I'm going to the kitchen to fix Josephine her favourite gingersnap cookies. Phone Kelly and see if she and her parents can come over. Tell Kelly that we're going to have a singsong and ask her if her parents can bring their fiddles. After that, I want you to phone Bill and Ross to invite them to join us. Maybe the sound of music will encourage Josephine to hurry back because you know something Frank, that kid is going to get the biggest hug and kiss that she's ever had!"

Ruth disappeared inside the house and walked quickly into the kitchen. Dr. Brown and Ron watched Ruth hurry by them, then got up out of their chairs, glanced at each other and walked over to the front door. They peered out of the door with puzzled looks on their faces at Frank who stood grinning and shaking his head.

Frank commanded, "Boys, you heard the lady. We're going to have some music and cookies. Get your instruments ready because we are going to have us a singsong. I'm going to phone over to Kelly's house right now."

Ron and Dr. Brown continued staring at him.

"You heard me, guys. Ron Latimer, get going on tuning up that banjo. Gene, you can play my electronic keyboard."

Gene Brown ignored Frank as he, followed by Ron, walked out the front door and came to a stop on the front lawn. He stroked his beard thoughtfully as he turned to look at Ron and Frank.

"Ron, it's great that your memory has returned. Think about the accident for a minute, and think about what exactly occurred."

"I know I killed my wife by entering the highway when it was unsafe to do so."

"Do you remember looking both ways before you drove onto the highway?"

"Yes. I have relived that accident countless times. I remember glancing right and left as I approached the highway, but I saw no one. Then, oh my God, there was this horrendous deafening noise. It was my fault that my poor Sandra was killed."

"Ron, the police report stated that those semi-trucks were well in excess of the speed limit. The road dips right there at the corner. By tracing the skid marks of the trucks, the police said that even if you hadn't been there, the trucks would have crossed the middle line and collided. It was a tragic series of events, Ron, which just happened. Now, Frank, I think the happy sounds of a singsong will help in enticing Josephine to return. We all know how much she loves music. Sometimes, Ron, when two people are grieving, they need to come together and share their feelings."

Ron stood motionless for a few minutes. Then, he began to walk slowly toward the hill as he glanced up toward Josephine and Rosy.

Gene Brown turned toward Frank, "Don't worry, Frank, I think that they will be all right. Now, if you would show me how to work that keyboard, we'll get started making music."

Standing on the hill, Josephine could hear the sounds of music drifting upward. She listened to the voices singing, *You Are My Sunshine* and then *Brahms' Lullaby*. Tears flowed down her cheeks as she threw herself face forward onto the grass and her body went limp. Images of a beautiful woman with sandy hair flashed into her mind.

Then Josephine felt a hand caressing her long hair.

"My sweet Josephine, I love you. It was an accident—you mustn't blame yourself for Sandra's death."

"Daddy Ron, if it hadn't been for me, mom would be alive!"

"No, Josephine. Dr. Brown has explained to me that the accident was just that, an unfortunate series of incidents that tragically led to Sandra's death. I want you to talk to him for a few minutes when we return to the house. Ruth and Frank love you. Look down toward the house, they are waiting for you. Let's go down and join the others."

Slowly Josephine sat up. She removed the locket that she had worn for so many years from her neck. Twisting the back in an anti-clockwise motion, it sprung open. She stared at her mother's face in the picture inside.

"Josephine, when I look at you I see so much of Sandra. Your musical talent, your kindness to others and your shy loving ways are all just like your mom's. It causes my heart to ache, Josephine, but I'm happy too because Sandra lives on through you, our precious daughter."

Josephine leaned over to Rosy and gave her a hug. The old dog's tail started to thump on the ground as she looked up at her. Then Josephine reached for Ron's hands. She and Ron stared into each other's eyes for a long moment, feeling the warmth touch their hearts. Then, hand in hand, Josephine and Ron walked down the hill, past the Care Centre and home.

STEEL FRIENDS

In 1944, the Lord Strathcona Armoured Regiment was slowly advancing along a narrow road that paralleled a crystal clear mountain stream. The stream meandered back and forth across a trough-shaped valley. Colonel Wainright, commander of the regiment, raised his hand bringing the armoured column to a stop. A tall man of formidable stature, he leaped down from his Sherman Tank and walked briskly to the edge of the stream. Wainright raised his binoculars to his eyes and attempted to see through the fog that hung over the verdant fields that were interspersed with patches of coniferous forest. Suddenly, emerging from the fog, he saw a large contingent of German Tiger Tanks that looked like grey phantoms moving rapidly toward him.

Wainright quickly returned to his tank and commanded his men to be ready to move instantly. The German Tigers increased their speed and formed a long line of moving weapons of destruction across the valley. Like the rumbling sound of an approaching thunderstorm, the German Tanks began firing their 88-millimetre guns as they paralleled the stream that curved out of the east, across the valley's road toward the north slope. When the Tigers had ascended the northern slopes of the valley, they turned, churning up the ground and creating huge dust clouds as they raced back toward the road. Wainright ordered his tanks to copy the Germans' tactics, and to commence firing with their 76-millimetre guns. Neither group made any attempt to cross the stream that separated them. Thunderous roars echoed throughout the valley as the two groups of tanks constantly moved back and forth across the valley. Main guns spat fire as they lobbed shell after shell. However, minimal damage was inflicted on either side as the gunners found it difficult to zero in on the moving targets.

The radio operator in Wainright's Sherman Tank listened for a moment to his headphones, and then turned to his Colonel.

"Begging your pardon, sir, but a Colonel Otto Schulz is requesting a ceasefire. Says he would like to talk to you."

"Sergeant, order our tanks to come to a halt and cease firing."

"Yes, sir!"

Wainright watched the German Tigers as they began to line up along the eastern edge of the stream.

The Sergeant listened intently to the radio and then relayed another message to his Colonel.

"Sir, Colonel Schulz is requesting that all tanks turn their guns to the rear in two minutes."

"Sergeant, issue an order that our tanks are to assume identical positions to the Tigers. As the Tigers rotate their guns to the rear, we are to copy their movements exactly."

"Yes, sir!"

Jumping off his tank, the fall leaves crackled under his feet as Wainright strode over to the bank of the stream. Motioning with his right hand, he directed the driver of his Sherman Tank to maneuver the 40-ton vehicle to the edge of the water. He then climbed back up on top of his tank and stared across the small stream at the German Tigers. The huge grey Tiger Tanks, as well as the thick groves of trees, now lined the eastern side of the stream. Staring back at him through a pair of binoculars was a lone figure dressed in the grey uniform of a Colonel of a German Armoured Regiment, who was standing in front of a battle-scarred Tiger Tank.

The figure from across the stream turned and picked up a small folding table and a knapsack. He proceeded to walk briskly in front of his German Tigers until he reached the bridge. Setting up the table on the bridge, he laid out a plate on which he placed some biscuits. He then removed a small kerosene burner. Next, a teapot was produced from the knapsack. The German Colonel then took a small pot down to the stream and filled it with water. He put the pot on the kerosene burner and soon the water was boiling. Then he picked up a tea bag. Wainright smiled and turned to his Sergeant.

"Sergeant, I have been invited to tea. Dig out the baking that my wife sent over to us. I certainly don't want to go empty-handed."

"Yes, sir. Sir, I will request a detail of our men to accompany you."

"No, Sergeant, that will not be necessary. Colonel Schulz wishes to have tea with me, alone, otherwise his ranking officers would accompany him. Don't worry, Sergeant. I will be fine. Sergeant, the men may exchange pleasantries and goods with the Germans, one tank crew at a time."

Wainright slung up his knapsack over his broad shoulder and walked briskly in front of his tanks to the bridge. The Canadian tank crews watched intently as Wainright marched by them and onto the bridge. Colonel Schulz stood and saluted Wainright as he approached. Wainright smartly returned the salute. The two men then sat down at the little wooden table and began silently drinking their tea.

Finally, Colonel Schulz leaned back in his chair and stared at Wainright. "Colonel Wainright, you have received two battlefield promotions since you have come to Germany. I was groomed to become an officer."

"I think, Colonel Schulz, that my commander needed a live person to fill the position."

"Perhaps, but then again, your commander must have had some good reasons for granting you the rank of Colonel."

"I think I am lucky to have extremely fine Canadian Soldiers under my command."

"Yes, I too am lucky. My Tigers are operated by some of the finest German soldiers of the Fatherland."

"It would appear that we have every right to be proud of our regiments."

"Yes, Colonel Wainright, and now I must return to my men as I am sure you are anxious to return to yours. Good day, Colonel Wainright."

"Good day, Colonel Schulz."

Over the next year, the two men managed to come together for tea on a few more occasions. These teas always seem to occur after a memorable battle, but the men never discussed the battles at their meetings. They would simply sit and have their tea, then, after exchanging a few comments, they would return to their regiments.

One day in June 1945, an event happened that had a profound effect on Wainright and Schulz's futures. In the early hours, four figures stood quietly at the edge of their alpine village gazing westward through the dissipating fog across a valley that was similar, but subtly different from the valley in which Wainright and Schulz had first met. On the two long sides and at the end of this valley, where the village was nestled, were walls of seemingly impenetrable mountains. The figures continued to look down the valley until they focussed on distant moving gray hulks, which they knew, were the dreaded enemy's tanks of destruction.

Carla Schulz stared down at her two small children who hugged her legs. Eyes filled with fierce pride, Carla spoke in a soft reassuring voice, "Anna, Kurt, you will stand straight and tall. Do not disgrace your papa and me by hiding behind me."

Anna stared wide-eyed at her mother and

father. "Mama, Papa, I am scared!"

Kurt spoke up in a tone of derision. "Well, I am a soldier like papa and I am not afraid." But Kurt did not move from his position behind Anna's leg.

"Children," whispered Carla. "We are all scared, but our enemy must not know."

"Come, stand between your mother and me." Otto's eyes radiated confidence as his deep voice spoke to his children.

Kurt stepped forward and clutched his father's hand. Anna took her mother's hand and stood tearfully looking at the oncoming enemy. Carla stared up at her husband's face. He took the pair of powerful binoculars that were hanging around his neck and peered through them at the oncoming tanks. His thin lips momentarily curled into the merest wisp of a smile that was quickly replaced by the dour demeanour of a wily military leader. Putting down the binoculars, Otto slowly removed his peaked cap. He stared at the two insignias on the front and gently ran his fingers over them. Removing his Luger from its holster, he took Carla's hand and laid the weapon into it. Then he knelt in front of his wife and children.

His deep blue eyes locked with Carla's as he whispered to her, "Carla, this insane war is almost over in one way or another for us. When the coming battle is done, the enemy will come to our house. If a Canadian Colonel named Alex Wainright knocks on our door and requests that you go with him, then you are to be cooperative. Colonel

Wainright is a man of honour. He will take care of you and the children. If anyone else other than Colonel Wainright knocks on our door, you are to bring everything to an end. Do you understand what I am saying, Carla?"

"Yes, Otto. Isn't it Colonel Wainright who commands the Canadian Regiment your tanks have fought against through France and our country?"

"Yes."

"Is he the man that you have had tea with during the ceasefires?"

"Yes, my dear."

"But is he not also the man who has given you your greatest battles?"

"Yes, Carla. Colonel Wainright of the Lord Strathcona Armoured Regiment is a tactical genius. His knowledge of the capabilities of his Sherman Tanks is superb. He understands the strengths of mobile armour. It has been an honour matching wits against him. Knowing Colonel Alex Wainright has been one of the few pleasures I have derived from this despicable example of a war. It is too bad that he is not German. I would have been proud to call him my friend and colleague-in-arms. It will be enough for me that you, Kurt, and Anna are delivered to safety."

Hugging each of his family in turn, Colonel Otto Schulz then stood, clicked his heels and saluted his family. He placed his hat on Kurt's head, and picked up Anna who buried her head into his broad shoulder. Leaning over, he gently tilted his wife's head upward to his. Otto then softly kissed Carla and lovingly caressed her long blonde hair. He straightened, put Anna gently down on the ground and then spoke a series of sharp commands into a radio hanging on his shoulder.

In the village a solitary church bell began to ring. The ground shook and the throbbing sound of powerful engines could be heard as fifty Panzerkampfwagen VI Tiger II tanks emptied out of the village and rumbled into view. The lead tank stopped six metres from Otto's feet and the tank commander smartly saluted Colonel Schulz. Carla's eyes filled with tears as she looked beseechingly upward, for perhaps the last time, into the eyes of her husband.

Her voice was filled with grief as she spoke in a trembling voice, "Otto, don't go. Stay with us."

"I'm sorry, Carla. I can't. I must go to meet our enemy."

Otto wheeled and strode over to the lead tank. He climbed into the tank and uttered a curt command to the driver. Otto raised his right hand to his brow as the Tiger Tank rolled past his family and then he was quickly gone, out of sight. A single tear rolled down Kurt's cheeks as he quietly raised his right hand to return his father's salute. Then Carla and the children slowly walked back to their home to await their fate.

The tanks the Schulz family had been watching, came to a halt on the westward side of the last bridge that spanned the stream one half kilometre before the road entered the village.

Colonel Alex Wainright climbed down off of his Sherman Tank and walked briskly to the edge of the stream. He looked through his binoculars at the distant village. Bands of morning fog continued to partially mask the village from view. Only the highest steeples of the taller buildings were visible. He observed a large contingent of German Tiger Tanks emerging from the fog. They advanced toward the Sherman Tanks in a V-formation. Alex quickly climbed back onto his tank and ordered his men to spread their tanks across the valley. He ordered his tanks to follow each other, and to traverse the valley in a circular pattern. They were only to commence firing on his orders.

Nearing the Shermans, the Tiger Tanks turned so that they were moving parallel to the stream. Then, they turned and moved toward the bank of the stream. As they were moving forward toward the Sherman tanks, their big guns began to slowly swivel toward the rear.

Wainright's radio operator listened intently and then reported to his Colonel.

"Sir, Colonel Schulz is requesting that all tanks turn their guns to the rear in two minutes."

"Sergeant, issue an order that our tanks are to assume identical positions to the Tigers. As the Tigers rotate their guns to the rear, we are to copy their movements exactly."

"Yes, sir."

Wainright thought to himself, *'Well my old friend and adversary, why are we here? We have fought across Europe since the Normandy Inva-*

sion. You wily devil, you have trapped us many times, but have never been trapped before. What is your real purpose in allowing us to trap you in this valley? Behind you are the mountains and that distant village. Your back is against the proverbial wall. Schulz, I can't believe you have done this.'

The buildings of the German village and the peaks of the mountains could now be seen clearly in the far distance. The solitary church bell continued to ring its solemn litany.

The two tank forces came to a halt not twelve metres from each other. Colonel Schulz climbed down from his tank, carrying his small folding table and knapsack.

Wainright watched Schulz, as he had on other occasions, make preparations for their tea.

"Sergeant dig out some of our good Canadian biscuits. I can't go to tea without taking something."

"But, sir, are you sure that you can trust him?"

"Sergeant, there is a time for battle and a time to talk. Warriors such as our friend over there, and I, know the difference. Now, dig out those sweets."

"Yes, sir!"

"Sergeant, as always, one crew at a time may meet the Germans at the stream to exchange cigarettes and pleasantries."

Colonel Wainright picked up his knapsack, turned and walked along the shore of the stream until he reached the bridge. He walked up to the little wooden table, saluted Colonel Schulz and shook hands. The two men then sat down at the table and quietly drank their tea. Not a word was spoken until the last biscuit was eaten, and the tea was drunk.

Then Wainright spoke in a solemn voice. "Colonel Schulz, your regiment is boxed in by those mountains. Why did you allow us to put you in this position?"

"My men and I fight better when in such a position."

"We will destroy your Tigers."

The slight smile appeared on Schulz's face. "Perhaps, but then again, perhaps not."

"Interesting that you chose to meet us in this valley and not in the streets of that village. Why not fight under the cover of those buildings?"

"Indeed, Colonel Wainright, why would that be?"

Wainright stood and looked toward the village for a few minutes. Then he turned back to look at Colonel Schulz who had continued to sit.

"You know, Colonel Schulz, this may well be your last battle. Casualties are bound to be heavy on both sides. I will miss our conversations. It is too bad that it has to end this way."

"Colonel Wainright, when the battle is done—I request that you go to the village. I have spoken to the mayor. It has been agreed that you, personally, accompanied by your officers and the mayor, are to go to each house and speak to the families. If you follow this request, then I guarantee there will be no resistance. The mayor waits to welcome you and your men."

"Colonel Schulz, you are a fine military commander who has always been most considerate of civilians' safety, but why would you have a particular concern about this village?"

"Many of my men have relatives in that village."

"And you, Colonel Schulz? Do you have relatives in that village?"

"Yes, but as the commanding officer of my regiment, it is my primary responsibility to care for my men as it is yours to care for your men. Is that not true?"

"Yes, Colonel Schulz, that is true.

"Colonel Wainright, I will not surrender my men to the Americans or Russians."

Wainright sat down at the small wooden table and looked intently into Schulz's eyes. He watched as Schulz's men went to the stream to exchange cigarettes and visit with his men.

Wainright continued to watch the men as he spoke, "Our men seem to enjoy talking to each other."

Schulz's eyes focussed on the men as he said, "Soldiers of integrity and honour, no matter on whose side they fight, have a great deal in common and understand each other. Colonel Wainright, I would only surrender to such a soldier."

"I would consider your surrender as an honour to my men and myself. If that is the choice you make, please give me time to inform headquarters. Colonel Schulz, please be assured, I will comply in every way with your request as to how my men and I enter your village."

Later, fifty German Tiger Tanks flanked and led by Colonel Wainright's Sherman Tanks, the Tigers' guns turned to the rear, rolled into the headquarters of a startled allied lieutenant general. Colonel Schulz and his men were treated with great respect as prisoners-of-war, and housed in a light security camp. Colonel Wainright shook hands with Colonel Schulz and the two men parted.

Little did Alex Wainright know that his path would eventually cross Otto Schulz's again.

* * *

In 1950 after Alex had attended the Remembrance Day ceremonies at Central Park in Calgary, he solemnly drove home to his bungalow in the district of Capital Hill. His wife, Meg, met him at the front door and quietly reached up to kiss him on the cheek. Alex walked over to their front room window. His steely eyes looked off into the distance toward the foothills of Calgary and his lips curved downward into a frown. Later, as always on this most nostalgic sad day, Meg got the car out of the garage and drove them to Bowness Park. Arriving at the park, she parked the car. Alex took their cooler over to the couple's favourite spot near a huge old pine tree.

As Alex stood looking toward the Bow River, he spoke in quiet, emotionally charged tones,

"Meg, I'm going for a walk over to the bridge."

"Okay, Alex."

Meg watched as Alex slowly walked toward the bridge. His head was bent and his massive shoulders sloped forward.

She thought, *'Alex, my love, go to the bridge. Think of the names and faces of the young men that were lost from your regiment. Remember the good times you had matching wits with wily old Otto. Later, we shall toast their memories with a glass of wine.'*

Alex wandered over to the Nose Hill Bridge that spanned the Bow River. He stood staring up the trough-shaped Bow River Valley toward Cochrane. In his mind, he could see his Sherman Tanks and the Tigers lined up along the banks of the little stream, the big guns facing the rear, and men of the two regiments meeting at the stream. On the bridge, he could see himself exchanging cryptic comments with Otto and the two of them sipping tea.

Suddenly, a familiar voice from the past interrupted his reverie.

"Alex, this Bow River Valley is most similar to my home valley in Germany—is it not?"

Quickly turning his head, Alex found himself staring into Otto Schulz's eyes. Otto snapped to attention and saluted Alex who then returned the salute. The two men studied each other for a few moments, then turned to stand side by side. Several minutes passed by and not a word was spoken.

Finally, Alex asked, "When did you come

to Canada?"

"Carla, the children, and I landed six months ago."

"Otto, I can't believe I'm seeing you again!"

"I couldn't believe my eyes when I saw you standing here either."

Observing the medals on Alex's broad chest, Otto's voice took on a reverent tone. "It is good that you take the time to remember."

"Our men were most special, Otto. We must remember and keep them alive."

"I do, here, next to my heart."

Otto opened his jacket and attached to his inside pocket were his medals.

"Otto, your medals should be worn proudly for all to see."

"No, Alex, it is too soon."

The two men stood silently staring up the valley toward the beautiful hills and the Rocky Mountains. Then Alex smiled and spoke.

"Otto, remember our last tea together?"

"Yes. It would be good to have tea together again."

"Remember, it was on a Wednesday. Even our final ceasefire was on a Wednesday."

"Yes, Alex. Wednesday noon hours would be a good time to have tea. Shall we meet at the Dooselberg next Wednesday? I will instruct the waiter to serve you some good German food."

"Okay, Otto, but the following Wednesday I will meet you at Oscar's. They have some fantastic Alberta Prime Beefsteaks. Come now and

I will introduce you to my wife, Meg."

"Alex...Carla and my children are right over there near that big group of trees."

"Otto, Meg is sitting right next to your family!"

The two men walked over to where Carla and Meg were sitting. When Carla saw them coming, she jumped to her feet and walked quickly over to embrace Alex, her long blonde hair flowing behind her. Close behind her walked Meg.

Carla said, "Thank you, Alex. If it weren't for you, we wouldn't be here."

"I'm glad I could help, Carla, but much of what happened would not have been possible without Otto's influence."

Alex's face turned red as Meg walked up and stood beside him. The two men introduced their family members. Meg took Alex's hand in hers.

She grinned up at him and gave him a kiss as she whispered, "I'm very proud of you, Alex."

In the coming weeks, the two men settled into a pattern of meeting at the two restaurants. One day while they were sitting quietly sipping their tea after lunch, Otto noticed that Alex had brought a tube of plans with him. He had expressed some curiousity about them and Alex had shown them to him. The plans were for an ice hockey stadium. Alex's architectural firm was competing to get the contract to build it for the City of Calgary. He told Otto that it was the biggest job his firm had ever competed for. Otto studied the plans and a frown formed on his face. Alex said he knew the plans needed to be finalized, and there were still details to be worked out.

Otto didn't speak a word, but simply sat and drank some more tea.

"Otto, what are your plans for the future?" continued Alex.

"Right now, I work in an office so that I can feed my family. In the future, I will take examinations here, so that I will become as I was before the war, an architect. I wish to again to be a builder and not a destroyer."

"Will you have to take courses to become an architect in Alberta?"

"The Architectural Association and the University of Calgary both have given me special permission to write their examinations. However, I want to take a few courses at the university first, to become familiar with the building needs in this area. When I have finished these things in a few months, I will start my own firm."

"Otto, I will be glad to help you with funds to start your firm. Also, I can put you in contact with several contractors as well as some potential customers to get your business rolling."

"Nein, Alex, not necessary! Good day!"

Alex sat and watched incredulously as Otto marched out of the restaurant slamming the door behind him.

That evening, Otto sat looking out of the kitchen window of his and Carla's modest house. He had come home from work and not spoken a word. He had sat through supper hardly touching his food. Then Kurt, Anna, and Carla had cleared the dishes. The children had left the kitchen at a subtle gesture from their mother. At last, Carla sat down opposite Otto and waited.

Finally, Otto looked into Carla's eyes. "Carla, today I had tea with Alex."

"I know, Otto. You have tea with Alex every Wednesday noon."

"No more!"

"What do you mean no more?"

"No more will I have tea with Alex."

"How come? What happened?"

"He insulted you, the children and me!"

"I don't understand, Otto. Alex wouldn't do such a thing."

"He was going to give us charity."

"What do you mean?"

"He said he would provide, what do you call it, capital and contacts for my architectural business. I don't need his help. I will get there on my own or not at all."

"Otto, Alex is a kind man, I'm sure that he meant no harm."

"Carla, there is one more problem."

"What is it?"

"Alex is in trouble."

"What do you mean?"

"He was showing me plans that he is going to present to a committee for an ice hockey stadium that the City of Calgary wishes to build. Alex said that his company has a great deal of money invested into that project, and it would mean a great deal if he wins the contract. The concept is superb, but the supporting structures are badly planned. Carla, he will fail in his bid unless those deficiencies are corrected. I don't know how to help him without insulting him."

"Yes, you do, Otto. You will find a way to help Alex without injuring his pride."

Carla rose from her chair and walked around the table to give Otto a kiss.

She smiled. "I will be waiting in bed for you."

As Carla walked down the hall, she thought to herself, 'Otto and Alex are so much alike. They are proud and good men, but both of them find it so difficult to accept help because they think they will then lose control. It will be interesting to see how they work out this situation.'

At one o'clock that evening in the Wainright house, a single light shone in the front room as Alex sat on the couch by himself looking out of the large picture window. Meg dressed in her satin house-coat silently walked into the room.

"Alex, what is the matter? Come to bed, darling. It's one clock in the morning. You have been staring out of that window for two hours."

Alex sat quietly, his chin resting on his hands. He turned and gazed deeply into his wife's lovely green eyes, then slowly turned back toward the window. His mouth twitched and then finally he looked back at his beloved Meg.

"Meg, I want to help Otto start his architectural firm. The man is brilliant, but he's just too darn stubborn to accept any help. He'll be years before he scrapes together the capital he needs just to get going. At our luncheon today, I tried to give him some ideas, and I offered him some help, but I think he feels I insulted him. He says he knows what he's doing and he doesn't need any charity. After that, he jumped to his feet and marched out of the restaurant. My God, Meg, you would think that after all he and I were through in the war, he would let me into his life. Why the devil does he have to be so pigheaded?"

Meg's lovely full lips curled upward into a smile as she silently cuddled up to her husband. She laid her head back on Alex's shoulder. His huge hands engulfed hers as they rested on her stomach. Alex looked down at Meg and she tilted her head upward to give him a kiss.

Alex turned and went back to staring out of the window as he spoke. "Well, Meg."

"Well, what?"

"Well, why are you grinning?"

"I love you, Alex."

"I know that, Meg, but why are you grinning?"

Meg shifted her position on the couch. She tucked her legs up under her. Her eyes danced as she spoke, "Alex, when you came home from the war you told me that you dreamed of opening your own architectural firm. My dad owned this city's largest firm. He tried to offer you some help, but you got angry and said that you were going to make it on your own."

"Well, I did make it on my own!"

"Did you?"

"Yes!"

"What happened after you drove all over the city delivering those business cards, posters, and flyers that we made in the basement?"

"Well, they did the trick because I started to get calls. Most people said they were glad that I was open for business and it was nice to deal with somebody who wanted to work on the smaller jobs."

"Alex, who do you think directed those people to you?"

"Meg, I can't believe your dad would have meddled in my affairs. It shows that he had no confidence in your husband."

"No, my dear! It shows that dad had every confidence in you, otherwise, he wouldn't have sent you those jobs. Don't forget by recommending you to those people, he put his own reputation on the line! He opened some doors for you and supported you in so many different ways, Alex, but he did it behind the scenes because he knew you were too pigheaded to accept the help up front. I know from talking to Carla that you and Otto are both very proud men. Perhaps you need to be like dad, and find a way to help Otto in a less obvious fashion."

"Meg, I never thanked your dad before he passed away. I didn't know."

"I know, Alex, but your success was thanks enough for dad. Come, Alex, I want you on your feet and heading for bed. I never did enjoy sleeping alone in that big bed."

Alex grinned and leaped to his feet. He saluted Meg and scooped her into his arms.

"Yes, ma'am!

The next Wednesday noon hour arrived, and both men showed up at Oscar's for their weekly tea. Neither man spoke a word as the hostess showed them to their usual table. The hostess hung up their coats in the coatroom.

Finally, Alex looked at Otto. "I thought perhaps I might be eating alone."

"I thought the same thing, but here we are."

"Otto, I apologize if I hurt your feelings last Wednesday. I am sure that you will start your firm and be very successful.

"I accept your apology. Have you worked out the details for the new stadium?"

"No, I guess I will be putting in some long evenings. Otto, if you will excuse me, I must make a phone call to my office."

Otto watched as Alex walked to the front of the restaurant. When he returned, the men ate their meals, then stood and shook hands. After they had collected their coats, they left the restaurant and headed back to their respective offices.

Arriving at his office, Otto was just in the process of hanging up his coat when he noticed the top of a white envelope sticking out of his inside pocket. He removed it and tore it open. Inside, he found a certified cashier's cheque for twenty thousand dollars. A slight smile crossed his face as he thought, *'I know you did this, my Canadian friend, but you will deny it! Of course, you will say that you had nothing to do with it! Thank you, my friend.'*

At about the same time, Alex was removing his coat at his architectural firm. His secretary looked up from her desk. "Alex, a courier brought this tube while you were out. He wouldn't say who it was from."

"Thank you, Dora," Alex said.

He took the tube and walked into his office. Closing the door quietly, he quickly opened the tube and smiled as he saw a set of the stadium's plans. He spread the plans out on his drafting table. Several suggestions for structural improvements were neatly printed on the plans. Alex grinned and chuckled to himself. He turned to look out of his office window and thought, *'Otto, you sly old fox, how did you obtain a copy of my plans? You have just saved me thousands of dollars in planning time! It seems that while I was trying to find a way around your pride to help you start your firm, you were trying to find a way around me to ensure the survival of mine! Thank you, my friend.'*

Friendship is a special bond.
It drives us to find ways to help
Our friends when they are in need.

THE ARROWS OF JUSTICE

One evening in September of 1992, Belle and Jess Gantry and their six children drove to the neighbouring ranch to visit their close friends, the Legares. Pulling into the driveway, they were naturally expecting to see Simon and Lorelei, and their son, Johnny, who would be running out to welcome them. As Jess slowed their Dodge Ram Charger, he noted the front door of the house was wide open and then he noticed the torn screen door. Looking at his wife in shock, he quietly ordered everyone to stay in the truck. The children heard their father's strange order, and they suddenly became aware of the tension in their parents. Immediately they were silent. As Jess opened the truck door, an eerie stillness seemed to pervade the surroundings. Slowly and cautiously, he approached the ranch house and stepped inside. All eyes were riveted on the torn screen door. Seconds ticked by as the family sat in stunned silence.

When Jess entered the front room, his eyes widened in horror. There on the carpet lay the blood-soaked bodies of Simon and Lorelei Legare. Between them sat twelve-year-old Johnny, in his pyjamas, his long, dark hair completely dishevelled. He was clenching one of his parents' hands in each of his, and staring out through the window upward toward the sky. Jess immediately ran back to his truck and used his cellphone to notify the Strathmore RCMP detachment.

Five minutes later, as Belle and Jess stood on the front steps and their six children huddled in the truck, a lengthy trail of dust appeared above the gravel road leading to the Legare's ranch. As the dust settled, an expressionless Sergeant Darryl Stewart arrived and skilfully brought his squad car, siren wailing and lights flashing, to a screeching halt in front of the ranch house. Two more squad cars and an ambulance wheeled in beside Darryl Stewart's vehicle.

The officers and the paramedics hustled to catch up with the Sergeant as he entered the house. Jess and Belle followed the officers in. Johnny was still sitting mournfully between his mom and dad firmly holding their hands. At his bare feet lay a tattered pencil drawing showing a seemingly meaningless design surrounding the letters SR. Sergeant Stewart and his fellow officers attempted to question Johnny, but Johnny just stared, his eyes glazed over.

Evidence collected at the scene showed that his parents had been viciously slain by several shotgun blasts. Eventually, it was determined that the shotgun shells were fired from an ancient 12-gauge firing-pin shotgun. The firing-pin indentation had created an irregular triangular-shaped depression on the percussion caps of the several shotgun shells located at the scene.

A tall, grey-haired, tough, but kindly crisis worker named Helen Trottier was the next to arrive. After thirty years of experience with crisis cases, Helen didn't think that anything would ever again shock her, but the sight of the quiet, slim, grieving Cree boy sitting between his two slain parents sickened her, and she had to swallow hard to quell a feeling of nausea rising up in her throat.

She thought, '*Come on, Helen, keep control. You can't be of any help to this young man if you lose it.*'

Finally, after kneeling to examine shotgun pellets embedded in the wall, checking several shotgun shells, looking over Johnny's pencil design and examining the bodies of Johnny's parents, a grim-faced Sergeant Stewart slowly rose to his full wiry six feet. He squared his broad shoulders as his tired eyes locked with Helen's. In an almost inaudible whisper, he told her that she could take Johnny into protective custody. When Helen bent down to gently extend her hand to Johnny's, he unexpectedly reacted.

Johnny's voice cut through the stillness of the house as he shrieked, "Get your hands off me! Leave me alone! I'm not going anywhere. I'll bury my parents and then I'll find out who did this…as soon as I can remember. Why can't I remember? Oh, why can't I remember?!"

Sergeant Stewart squatted down beside Helen and quietly said in a firm, kindly voice, "Son, take it easy. Mrs. Trottier just wants to take you someplace where you will be safe."

Johnny vigorously shook his head. He hugged his knees to his chest and stared at the ceiling. Then he began to quietly chant a poem in Cree that Jess and Belle knew had been taught to him by his mother. A few minutes later, two of the Mounties moved quietly toward him. Johnny slowly stood up, staring menacingly at them. Sergeant Stewart motioned to the officers to move back. Then Jess and Belle moved quickly to break the tension.

Jess knelt and held his arms out to Johnny who immediately darted over to him. Jess wrapped his heavily-muscled arms around him. Belle tenderly wiped Johnny's tears as she softly spoke to him. She, like Jess, knelt in front of Johnny and gently placed her hands on his cheeks. Belle, with tears in her eyes, stared deeply into his dark, sad eyes. Then she looked over Johnny's head and stared questioningly into Helen's eyes. Helen nodded imperceptibly.

"Mrs. Trottier, could Johnny come and stay with us? Johnny's folks were fine people and wonderful friends. Would it be possible for us to take care of Johnny?"

"Mrs. Gantry, I met your six children out in your truck. Are you sure you want another child to care for?"

"Johnny is not just another child to care for—he is a friend of ours. Jess and I have shared many a happy time with him and his parents. He is a very special young man who would add to the love that we share as a family. Our kids—Michelle,

Tammy, Jillian, Russell, Andrew, and Jess Junior said to tell you that if Johnny didn't come to live with us, you would be in *real big* trouble."

Helen smiled as she replied, "Mr. and Mrs. Gantry, I sense that there is a warm loving home waiting for Johnny if he wishes it. Besides, I think I'm outnumbered eight to one on this issue. I will speak to my superiors, but I think it could be arranged if that's okay with Johnny."

Johnny slowly lifted his head and between sobs whispered, "Uncle Jess and Aunt Belle are my friends. Please let me go with them."

Two months later, a child psychiatrist at the Alberta Children's Hospital evaluated Johnny's emotional state. He reported his findings to Sergeant Stewart, Belle and Jess Gantry, Helen Trottier, and Roger Radonsky—the Strathmore School Principal. The psychiatrist, Dr. Terry McFadden, thoughtfully stroked his greying bewhiskered chin as he scanned a stack of Johnny's test results. He stated that when Johnny's emotions matured, he was confident that the boy would come to terms with his parents' death. At that point, there was the possibility that the memory of his parents' murderer would return. Johnny's file would remain open until the murderer had been found, arrested and convicted.

Three months after the death of Johnny's parents, Jess and Belle petitioned the courts and became Johnny's foster parents. One year later on September 15, 1993, Johnny's thirteenth birthday, Jess and Belle became his proud legal guardians.

Helen Trottier, Darryl Stewart, and Terry McFadden had all written enthusiastic letters of support to help Jess, Belle, and Johnny speed up the legal process.

Now, it was celebration time. The entire red-headed Gantry clan, dressed in their finest western wear of red shirts, black pants, black cowboy boots, and matching five-star, black Stetsons, held a steak barbecue and a lively country dance at their ranch. The entire community was invited to attend. Jess and Belle sent special invitations to Darryl Stewart, Helen Trottier, Terry McFadden, and Roger Radonsky to join them for this most special occasion.

Roger privately expressed surprise to Helen and Darryl that Johnny hadn't been sent by the Social Service authorities to live with a Cree Indian band.

Helen smiled as she quietly replied, "Mr. Radonsky, I agree with you that Johnny's cultural heritage is a most important factor. However, Johnny's emotional ties are centred on his deceased parents and on their ranch. Belle has assured me that she and Jess will ensure that Johnny has ample opportunity to enrich his native heritage. Besides, look how happy Johnny is square dancing the *Alabama Jubilee* with Michelle Gantry. Those two young people are really something! I wish I was young again and could move like that. Most important, however, is that the Gantry family loves Johnny and within that love, he will find happiness and security."

Roger Radonsky shook his head as he said, "Well, Mrs. Trottier, I don't feel that a native boy can fit into our society *and* the Cree society."

Smiling, Darryl commented, "It happens all the time, Roger. After all, I should know."

"What do you mean by that?"

"Never mind, Roger. You wouldn't believe it anyway."

Over the next three years, Jess took care of Johnny's land and all the proceeds were placed in a trust fund for his education. Belle and Jess, true to their promise to Helen Trottier, took Johnny and their children to native cultural events.

Huge, master rancher, ham-handed Jess regularly taught his children and Johnny the various aspects of becoming a successful rancher. Belle made sure that the seven children were heavily involved in the local 4-H club. The Gantry's front room bookshelf was soon covered with trophies and ribbons from 4-H competitions.

Sergeant Stewart when he was off duty would often visit the Gantry's ranch. He would, along with Jess and Belle and much to the delight of the children, give them lessons in archery, marksmanship, outdoor skills and orienteering. Johnny and Michelle proved to be exceptional students in all that Sergeant Stewart taught. His visits usually ended with stories told by the adults to the children. Large mugs of steaming hot chocolate with big fat marshmallows, accompanied by homemade cookies, were always passed around before the children settled down in front of the Gantry's massive, brownstone, family room fireplace. Belle, Jess, and Darryl noticed with some amusement that the children always left a space beside Johnny for Michelle.

One evening when Michelle was sick, she had stayed in her bed propped up by an enormous number of pillows rather than join the family in the family room. As the storytelling started, Jess watched Johnny stealthily leave the room. A few moments later, he quietly got up to go in search of Johnny. He found him sitting beside Michelle's open door reading to her from a book by her favourite author.

Jess smiled as he said, "Kids, would you like some company?"

Michelle grinned, her bright blue eyes dancing as she replied, "I have some company, Dad, but sure, the more the merrier."

Storytelling continued that evening with the entire family, Sergeant Stewart, and even Duke—the Gantry's Border Collie—crowded into Michelle's bedroom.

As Johnny was growing up on the Gantry's ranch, the only reoccurring problem centred on his being overprotective toward the Gantry family, and toward his pets. It seemed that he was always overreacting to situations if he thought anyone was either mistreating one of the Gantry kids or one of his pet animals. When tall, willowy, freckled-faced Michelle Gantry was eleven, she arrived home one day with her red hair matted with mud, sticks, and leaves. Johnny asked her what had happened. She stared at him through tear-filled eyes and told him that fourteen-year-old, lean, mean Len, Mr. Radonsky's son, had pushed her and then laughed at her as she fell headfirst into a mud puddle.

The next day as Len who always seemed to have a sneer on his face was swaggering home with his buddies from school, twelve-year-old Johnny stealthily followed at a distance. Suddenly, Johnny raced out from behind some dense bushes. Before Len's buddies could stop him, Johnny grabbed Len, lifted him above his head and threw him headfirst into a deep irrigation ditch. Len didn't stop screaming until he hit the water. Johnny ran off before Len's friends could catch him.

Len half-swam and half-stumbled out of the ditch. Then he immediately raced home and phoned his dad at the school. After speaking to Len, Roger Radonsky leaned back in his swivel chair, gazed thoughtfully out of the window and then phoned Jess Gantry. He informed Jess that Johnny would be suspended for five days over the incident. Jess and Belle strongly objected to the suspension on the grounds that they felt that Len had initiated the problem. The suspension was cancelled after Principal Radonsky, Jess, Belle, Johnny, Michelle, and Len had a meeting at the school regarding the incident. However, Roger did suggest that Jess and Belle consider enrolling Johnny in an Anger Management class in Calgary.

Later at home in the Gantry's spacious kitchen, Jess asked Johnny why he hadn't come to him about the problem.

Johnny quietly mumbled, "Nobody hurts my

family or my animals and gets away with it."

Belle gave Johnny a hug. She quietly whispered in his ear, "Honey, I'm sure Michelle appreciates your help, but there *are* better ways to solve problems."

Michelle and her sisters covertly glanced at each other as they finished wiping the supper dishes.

Over the next couple of years, Len Radonsky seemed to take great delight in annoying Johnny who would, of course, overreact to the provocation. After each incident, Principal Radonsky would again strongly suggest that Johnny be sent into Calgary to a special class. Finally, Jess put an end to it by refusing to allow Johnny to be anywhere near Len Radonsky. Jess and Belle decided that each evening they would sit down with the children for half-an-hour sharing the day's events and discussing different ways to solve problems.

At about this same time, somebody began to hunt on the Gantry's land without permission. Someone was constantly leaving the Gantry's gates open, bothering the livestock and diverting the irrigation water. Jess and Belle reported the incidents to Sergeant Stewart and the Ranchers' Association.

One day in town, Roger Radonsky saw Jess loading his truck. He pointedly walked over to him.

"Jess...I told Mrs. Trottier that you and Belle might have problems raising Johnny on your ranch. Now I understand that somebody, maybe even Johnny himself, is leaving your gates open, letting your livestock out and diverting your water."

Jess's large two-hundred-and-sixty-pound body seemed to block out the sun as he spun around to rivet his eyes on the much smaller Roger who quickly took a step backward.

In icy measured tones he growled, "Sergeant Stewart has kept it quiet about our problems. How do you know about them?"

"I hear about what goes on in town. After all, I am the school principal and I have a right to know."

* * *

At sixteen years of age, Johnny had a particularly disturbing dream. In it, he saw the terrifying image of an eyeless, hooded monster in black. In the monster's left hand was an old, double-barrelled shotgun whose barrels had twin wisps of smoke curling out of them.

A low, guttural, eerie voice seemed to penetrate into Johnny's mind.

'I just wanted some attention from your mom, but she always ignored me. Your mom was always so proud of being Cree. She thought she was better than me. Didn't think a mixed blood was good enough for her. I had to kill her. Your dad tackled me. He recognized me and I had to kill him, too. It wouldn't do for him to know who I was. Show yourself, Johnny. Where are you? Don't worry, Johnny—I'm your friend. I'll make it quick and painless.'

Johnny screamed out loud, "You killed my parents! You will kill no more!"

In the dream, Johnny slowly climbed out of his bed and confronted the monster in black. He reached deep within himself and found the courage to leap through the air toward the monster. Johnny reached for the black mask, but suddenly the monster dissolved. Then, in his dream, he felt two strong, loving hands resting gently on his shoulders and as he turned around, he found himself looking into the dark eyes of his mom and dad, Lorelei and Simon Legare.

Simon's long black hair seemed to glisten. He whispered in a low voice, '*No, Johnny. That is not the way! You must live! You are our heritage. You carry within you our hopes and dreams. Use the skills of our ancestors to lead our murderer into Sergeant Stewart's hands.*'

Deep concern and love seemed to radiate from Lorelei's dark eyes.

'*Johnny, we will not be going home to our final resting place until we have helped you and the Sergeant make things right. The monster in black must be brought to justice.*'

'*Mom, Dad...who is this monster in black? I feel that I know him, but I can't remember.*'

Suddenly, Johnny saw his mother and father begin to slowly fade from sight.

"No—don't leave me! Come back! Don't go!" Johnny screamed out loud as, in his dream, he ran after his parents.

Johnny woke from his vivid dream as he

bounced off his closed bedroom door with a bone-rattling crash and fell to the floor.

He scurried to his feet as he heard Jess's deep booming voice.

"I'm not waiting any longer, Belle. Kids, get back out of the way!"

Quickly Jess entered the room. Belle and their six kids literally spilled into the room behind him. Johnny found himself surrounded by a chorus of voices. A piercing whistle and a firm demand for quiet came from Jess, penetrating the confusion and silencing everyone present.

Jess stood there in his pyjamas, all six-foot-three of him, towering over Johnny. He placed a heavily-calloused hand on Johnny's shoulder and quietly asked, "Johnny, are you okay? We thought we heard a scream and then we heard a crash."

Belle urgently asked, "Johnny, honey, were you having a bad dream?"

"I'm okay. I thought the murderer and my mom and dad were here. I feel like I should recognize who murdered them...but I just can't remember."

Belle nodded her head solemnly. "You will, Johnny, you will."

"I don't know. It's been two years now since my mom and dad were killed. I'm scared. I've got to remember before the monster in black kills again. He's still out there someplace. What if he hurts you and the kids? Maybe I should just leave."

"Don't worry, Johnny. We Gantrys are made of pretty tough stuff. If we look out for each other, we'll be okay."

Michelle listened gravely to her parents and Johnny. Her thoughtful eyes gazed intently into Johnny's and he blushed, then looked away.

"Johnny, what did Aunt Lorelei and Uncle Simon say?" questioned Michelle.

"They said to use the skills of our ancestors to lead their murderer into Sergeant Darryl's hands."

The next day, Jess and Belle consulted with the psychiatrist, Terry McFadden, as well as with their family doctor about Johnny's nightmare. Both men told them that most likely Johnny's buried memories were starting to come forth into his consciousness and to be patient with him.

The next week, Terry and the doctor both curled at the same bonspiel in Strathmore. The two men privately discussed Johnny's case in a secluded corner assuming they were away from all other prying ears, but one very troubled person did manage to overhear the discussion. He made a fateful decision, then quietly went on about his business.

*   *   *

One evening about four years after the death of Johnny's parents, the land was cast into a strange scene of deep shadows that blended into the fading golden light of the sunset. The Gantry spread lay nestled in its U-shaped valley and peace appeared to prevail throughout. Two figures carrying hunting bows could be seen strolling alongside the shimmering lazy stream that wound its way like a snake across the Gantry spread, while their Border Collie, Duke, bounded excitedly all around them. The fall leaves covered the ground in a carpet of red, orange, and gold. Up and down the stream an abundance of ducks and geese practised taking off and landing with their young ones in preparation for their long trip to the south. As the two figures strolled along, the crackling and snapping of leaves could be heard.

Sixteen-year-old Johnny and fifteen-year-old Michelle had been sent by Jess to bring their prize Holstein dairy herd down from the north pasture for milking. Duke ran continually, barking excitedly in expectation of bringing the herd home.

Michelle and Johnny were a study in contrasts, both in appearance and in temperament. Michelle with her long red hair and freckled complexion was pretty, like her mother. Johnny had grown to be five-foot-eleven and was dark and lanky. His coal-black hair hung down to his shoulders and his keen dark eyes constantly scanned the area around them. Michelle was extremely talkative and outgoing. Johnny, by contrast, tended to keep his thoughts to himself and chose his words carefully when he spoke. Michelle was naturally bubbly and good-natured. Although Johnny wouldn't openly admit it, Michelle was like a shaft of light that penetrated the darker recesses of his soul. At his young age, Johnny didn't really think about their relationship as being love, he just knew that he enjoyed being with Michelle because she made him happy. Michelle, although a year younger than Johnny, already knew that someday she wanted Johnny to come to realize how special he was to her.

As the two young people approached the gate to the field, they found that someone had left it open again. Fresh vehicle tracks could be seen passing through the gateway and disappearing off into the distance parallel to the stream. Johnny laid his hunting bow on the ground. He squatted down and scanned the ground in front of him as well as the far horizon.

"Michelle, I would be willing to bet my prize heifer, Mia, that our mysterious friends are back on our land. Uncle Jess and Sergeant Darryl have tried a hundred times to catch those trespassers. I'll bet it's Len and his buddies. Len thinks he can go anywhere and do anything he wants just because he's the principal's son! He's always trying to give me a hard time whenever he has the chance."

"Johnny, dad told us to rule our actions with our heads not our fists. If we get angry, we'll just end up making a mess of things."

Johnny, his eyes studying the vehicle's tracks, quietly moved ahead of Michelle. Suddenly two sharp cracks echoed across the stillness of the vast land. Then an animal cried out in sheer terror. Behind Johnny, Michelle clutched her left shoulder.

Johnny's black eyes riveted in the direction of the gunshots and he screamed, "It's Mia! I know it's Mia!"

Bounding along the stream like a deer, Johnny quickly disappeared out of sight. Michelle slowly, painfully, gamely tried to keep up to Johnny, but the pain in her shoulder simply didn't allow her to catch up to her swift companion. Eventually when Michelle reached Johnny, she was saddened by what she found.

Johnny was knelling and trembling with rage, his hunting bow beside him, as tears streamed down his face. His arms were wrapped around the tan-coloured neck of Mia. The beautiful animal looked pleadingly into Johnny's eyes as she cried out in pain.

Glancing toward Michelle, Johnny gasped, "Michelle, you've been hurt! You've got blood all over your shoulder. I'm sorry I left you—I didn't realize you'd been hurt. Here, let me wrap your shoulder with my shirt. Look what's happened to Mia! She was scared by those shots and must have tripped in a badger hole. I don't think that her leg is broken though. How could duck hunters shoot that wildly? I'm going after them."

"No, Johnny, please cool down! Mia and I need you here. Use the cellphone and call my folks to come with help. Johnny…there's something odd about this situation. I think whoever did this wants you to go after them, but they have shotguns and you don't! Please call dad and mom."

Johnny suddenly stopped talking. He stood motionless and stared blankly at Michelle and Mia. Then he cried out in pain, squatted down and held his head in his hands.

Forgetting her own pain, Michelle went to Johnny and squatted down beside him. Duke nosed his way under Johnny's arms, laid his head on his lap and stared up at him.

Johnny murmured in a voice that seemed to come from far away, "The murderer has been trying to get rid of me for the last four years, but now I know who he is. Mia's bellowing, the blood on your shoulder and the sound of the shotgun made me remember."

"Johnny…this has got to be a set-up. The murderer must know that you will come after him. He's out there waiting for you. Stay here with me. We'll call dad and mom. If you attack him, he will kill you and claim it's self-defence."

"Michelle, you're a great friend, but the wrong done to my family can only be made right by me. Mom and dad will never take their final journey home until this wrong is righted."

"For crying out loud, let dad and Sergeant Darryl take care of it! Cool down and think! Think about how your mom and dad would want you to handle this problem."

Two more shotgun blasts cracked through the air and then a deathly silence descended on the dense clumps of trees and bushes skirting the banks of the stream. In the far distance, Michelle and Johnny could see the frightened herd milling aimlessly around the pasture.

"Michelle, I won't let that monster kill anyone that I love again! I will lead him away from you and Mia. I've dialled the number. Here, take the cell. Tell Aunt Belle and Uncle Jess what's happened."

"Johnny—don't go! Stay here. I need you."

Johnny stood up, picked up his bow and waited for someone to answer the phone. Then he turned and immediately disappeared into the woods. Michelle numbly watched Johnny go, and then she suddenly became aware of her mother's voice repeatedly saying, "Hello, is anyone there?"

Michelle's voice was choked with fear and anxiety. "Mom!"

"Michelle, what's the matter?"

"Mia's hurt and Johnny's gone and Mom…I've been shot!"

"What?!"

Michelle told her mom what had happened. Belle asked her to hold on while she quickly called her dad in from the barn.

Belle came back on the ranch telephone. "Michelle, dad's on his truck phone talking to Sergeant Darryl. Oh! Here's dad—he's just picking up the extension."

"Michelle, are you okay?"

"I guess so, Dad. Johnny's gone after the man who did this. He said he remembered who murdered his mom and dad. Dad…I'm afraid Johnny's going to get himself killed."

"Michelle, Johnny is most likely tracking the man as we speak. He has a quick temper, but he cools off just as quickly. Now, honey, take a deep breath and slowly tell me exactly where you and Mia are at the present moment."

After Michelle had described her location to her dad, there was silence for a moment. Then Jess spoke again.

"Listen, honey, it's possible that the man may be coming your way. He might have left his vehicle somewhere among the trees. If Mia can walk, take her among the trees and stay there until we arrive."

"Dad, I'm scared. Please hurry!"

"I know, honey, I know. Don't worry, mom and I are coming right now."

Fifteen minutes later, Jess, Belle, Sergeant Stewart, the veterinarian, Hank—the hired man, and the ambulance all arrived one after the other. Hank was driving the Gantry's one-ton farm truck with a horse trailer hitched behind it. Jess brought his truck to a halt in a swirl of dust. Immediately, Belle rushed over as the paramedics helped Michelle into the ambulance. The veterinarian jumped out of his vehicle and gave Mia a quick examination and a local anaesthetic. Then he wrapped some elastic bandage around her leg and loaded her into the horse trailer. Then Hank drove Mia back to the barn.

Michelle raised herself up on the gurney and tearfully stared at Jess and Darryl.

"Dad, Sergeant Darryl, please hurry and find Johnny. I heard shotgun blasts over there toward those trees while I was waiting for you to come."

Darryl Stewart stared at Michelle and quietly said, "Michelle, I know how you feel about

Johnny. Don't worry. I have an idea as to where we'll find him."

Jess waved to Michelle, and then watched as the ambulance left. Then he and Darryl set off to search along the stream. Eventually they found a Land Rover hidden in the bushes about a half kilometre upstream. The distributor cap and several wires had been removed from the engine. Further up the stream, Sergeant Stewart found an arrow sticking out of a birch tree. Shotgun pellets were found in two trees standing side by side. However, no sign of Johnny or anyone else could be seen in the dense woods.

Jess planted his huge hands on his hips. He whirled around and glared at Darryl, then quietly commented in a low growl, "Darryl, don't you know that Len and his buddies have been bothering Johnny for years?"

"I know, and I do understand, but Jess, I have to maintain the law."

"Yes, I know, Darryl, but it doesn't seem fair. Johnny has been doing so well in learning to deal with things and now this happens!"

"Jess, I believe that someone is trying to set Johnny up. Someone knows that he tends to go after those who hurt members of your family or the animals. Injuring Mia was bad enough, but shooting at Michelle...well, that was probably the last straw. Hopefully Johnny will have cooled down before he reaches anyone."

"I hope so, Darryl."

Earlier, a man dressed in black pants and

shirt and wearing a black ski mask had quietly waited in the deep underbrush for Johnny to appear. When the man heard the soft twang of a hunting arrow thudding into the birch tree above and to the left of his head, he whirled and shot in the direction the arrow had come from. The sound of the shot had echoed through the dense stand of birch trees growing along the bank of the stream, but then there was silence.

Suddenly, Johnny's voice could be heard. "I know you killed my parents! You will come with me to see Sergeant Darryl."

The man became aware of the sound of running feet and then he could see Johnny's figure rapidly disappearing across the field. Quickly he fired between the two birch trees in Johnny's direction, then he raced after him, but Johnny disappeared over the rim of the valley. As the man reached the barbed wire fence marking the end of the Gantry's property, an arrow thudded into the fence post beside him. Again he whirled and fired his shotgun. He slowly studied his surroundings in the failing light, but not a soul could be seen.

Eventually, the man walked over the rise and then he saw a group of familiar red buildings, several of which had the name *Legare* painted on their sides. He was now on the Legare Ranch where, so many years before, tragedy had struck down Johnny's parents. The man knew that he had made a grievous error in pursuing Johnny to his birthplace because he was afraid that this stressful situation might tear apart the barriers in Johnny's mind and cause him to remember the vivid details of that fatal evening four years ago.

The sun vanished below the horizon and a deep darkness descended upon the deserted ranch. Cautiously, the darkly attired man approached the ranch house. He stood quietly staring at the darkened building as the wind shrieked and moaned through the trees surrounding the perimeter of the yard. The ranch buildings cast long, deep, ebony shadows. In a window of the ranch house, a solitary kerosene light could be seen flickering and glimmering. The man watched as the drapes were slowly parted revealing the familiar face of a woman. Suddenly, an arrow coursed through the air burying itself with a quiver in a log at the man's feet. Looking around carefully, he squatted down and wrenched the arrow out of the log. A piece of paper was tied to it. On the paper was written, I REMEMBER WHAT YOU DID! He stared at the message, then at the woman.

"You're dead, Lorelei! It can't be you. You're dead!"

Slowly, he raised his shotgun and shot through the window. Lorelei stood smiling, and then slowly faded from the man's view. Another arrow thudded into the log. Again the man tore the message paper off the arrow. The message read, YOU WILL PAY FOR YOUR CRIMES, THEN WE WILL GO HOME. He studied the buildings and peered into the shadows, but not a living soul could be seen. A chilling wolf-like howl pierced the air and a solitary drum began to beat. Lorelei's image slowly reappeared in the window and she stood smiling, pointing an accusing finger at him.

He yelled, "All this native mumble-jumble won't spook me! They will never believe you over me, Johnny. Show yourself."

Another arrow thudded into the log a few metres from the man's feet.

In a strained voice touched with fear, he said, "For Pete's sake, Johnny, I tried to get you removed from this community, but you wouldn't go, would you? You insisted on living with Belle and Jess. Four years you have lived out here and each day I feared that someday you would remember."

Suddenly, the man was bathed in light from behind by the high beam of a powerful flashlight. Sergeant Darryl Stewart, his pistol held out in front of him in his right hand, ordered the man to drop his gun. As soon as he did, Jess ran rapidly out of the woods.

Jess, his steely grey eyes focussed on *the man in black*, reached out with a heavily-muscled arm, picked the man up off the ground and shook him like a plastic bag rustling in the wind.

Then he tore off the man's ski mask and bellowed, "Where's Johnny, Radonsky? You'll pay for this!"

"What do you mean, me? That trouble-maker has to be just around the corner of the barn. His arrows all came from that direction. Sergeant Stewart, tell this big oaf to put me down—he's assaulting me. I want you to arrest Johnny. He's been trying to kill me."

"Jess, would you please put Mr. Radonsky on the ground gently. Mr. Radonsky, you had better pray that Johnny's okay when we find him or I may be tempted to leave you here with Jess."

Jess opened his hand and dropped Roger Radonsky on the ground. He reached into his pocket, pulled out his cellphone and contacted Belle. He told her that he and Darryl were at the Legare ranch.

Darryl Stewart carefully examined Roger's shotgun. He studied the ornamental carving on the stock and the firing pin. Then he thoughtfully laid the gun in the trunk of his squad car. Darryl next proceeded to handcuff Roger, despite his sputtering protests, to an old pump.

Ten minutes later, Belle arrived after having driven at high speed in the Gantry's one-ton farm truck. Leaving her to watch Roger—Darryl and Jess proceeded to search the barn and the other buildings, but they found no trace of Johnny. Returning, Darryl released Roger from the pump and handcuffed his hands behind his back. Then they all went into the house. Roger was seated on the front room chesterfield with Jess and Belle watching him, while Darryl searched the basement, the main floor and the upstairs. No sign of Johnny was found. Suddenly, Belle's face lit up and she stared up at Darryl.

"When I've come here with Johnny before to help him do some chores, he's often sat and stared at the large walk-in master bedroom closet.

He told me it was a safe place. I would ask him why it was a safe place, but he always said that he couldn't remember."

Belle stood, smoothed back her long red hair and walked slowly over to the bedroom closet. She opened the door, but to her surprise, she didn't find Johnny. The men joined her and began rapping on the closet walls. Eventually, they heard a hollow sound and they discovered a sliding panel.

"Hello, Johnny. You can come out now", called Belle.

Johnny walked out into the bedroom and into Belle's arms.

* * *

Two days later, Sergeant Stewart requested that the Gantrys permit him to use their house to conduct interviews and to gather evidence as it was near at hand to the crime scene. He conducted interviews with Roger Radonsky, Johnny, and Michelle. Other officers from Strathmore were there to assist him. When Sergeant Stewart was finished, he sat busily flipping through the pages of his notebook, occasionally looking up in a contemplative manner. Sometimes he would request a point of clarification, but mostly he just sat quietly reading his notes. Having interviewed everyone individually, he began to look for inconsistencies in their stories. The family, Roger Radonsky, and the other officers waited quietly in the front room for him to continue.

Finally, Roger Radonsky could stand it no longer and he blurted out, "Sergeant Stewart, as the school principal and a respected member of this community, I think it's time I put an end to this farce. You know that Johnny is a troublemaker! He has been harassing my son for years. Johnny is a nice boy, but he just can't help being the way he is."

Johnny stared at Roger, his dark eyes seething with rage. "You've always just let Len hurt me and the other kids. I know you killed my mom and dad, and now you want to take me away from Aunt Belle and Uncle Jess. Instead of telling you up there in the woods that we had to go and see Sergeant Darryl, I should have just killed you!"

Roger shook his head and snorted, "Kill me! You're just a sixteen-year-old kid armed with a hunting bow who managed to hit a few trees. You've got it all wrong anyway."

Roger sat there with a smirk on his face.

Abruptly, Johnny leaped from his chair and tried to get at Roger. Sergeant Stewart and Jess quickly grabbed him and firmly seated him at the opposite end of the front room.

Michelle walked over to Johnny, leaned over and stared into his angry eyes. "Johnny, take it easy. What you just tried was not cool."

Michelle put her arms around Johnny and whispered, "Please, Johnny, settle down. Let the Sergeant do his job. I'm sure he will be fair."

Johnny blurted out; "Fat chance, Michelle! He looks at me and right away he decides that I can't be trusted."

Sergeant Stewart's fair complexion became ruddy as his intense eyes flashed with anger. He marched over to Johnny and started to address him in the *Cree* language.

"*My mother's family are of the Cherokee Nation. My father is white. I speak half-a-dozen native languages and various dialects. When I was your age, Johnny, I spent at least half of my time on an Oklahoma reservation. You will show respect for me personally, and for my uniform. I understand your feelings, but I want you to be quiet and let me conduct this investigation my way.*"

Johnny's mouth hung open. Then he gazed into Michelle's eyes. She smiled at him, hugged him and then grasped his hand. Johnny stared at the floor and quietly mumbled, "I'm sorry, Sergeant Darryl. I guess I messed up. I just want to make things right for my mom and dad."

"I know, Johnny, but you've got to trust in my integrity not only as an officer of the law, but also as your friend. Belle, Jess, Michelle, and the rest of the kids are on your side. Don't worry, you'll get a fair shake."

Sergeant Stewart turned and his grey eyes seemed to peer into the innermost depths of Roger Radonsky. "Johnny has been taught archery by me. Check the bookshelf, Mr. Radonsky. You will find numerous awards that Johnny has won for archery, orienteering, tracking and other sporting competitions. If he'd wanted to kill you, you would most assuredly be dead. Jess and I followed Michelle and

Johnny's tracks up to where we found Mia. Their tracks were in the open field, not in the trees alongside the stream. Therefore, you must have seen them when you shot. How do you explain those observations?"

Radonsky quietly muttered, "Well, all right. I saw them, but I was trying to shoot over their heads at some ducks."

Jess's face turned red.

"It sounds to me like you deliberately shot my daughter, Mr. Radonsky. If you don't answer to the law for what you have done, you will definitely have to answer to my family."

"Jess, please let me continue."

"Sorry, Darryl."

Sergeant Stewart shook his head, consulted his notes and then continued. "Mr. Radonsky, we have all agreed as to where you and Johnny were standing when you confronted each other. I found shotgun pellets buried in the trees to the left and to the right of Johnny's position. Please explain why you obviously shot at him."

"This troublemaker appeared between those trees and shot an arrow at me. I was protecting myself."

"Mr. Radonsky, I checked the angle of the arrow's flight. Johnny couldn't have shot that arrow as it came from your left side, not from in front of you. I would now ask that you to examine the arrows that are placed on the dining room table. I collected them from between the stream and Johnny's parents' ranch house. Compare those arrows to Johnny and Michelle's arrows. Jess, would you pass the kids' quivers to Mr. Radonsky."

After a few moments, Sergeant Stewart continued, "Mr. Radonsky, please tell me what you observe."

Roger Radonsky examined each of the arrows. Finally, he looked up and stated, "The markings are different. And the hunting arrows found in the trees are handmade wooden arrows—the kids' arrows are made of fibreglass."

"That is correct, Mr. Radonsky. These arrows didn't come from any store in Strathmore or any other local community. They are not manufactured fibreglass arrows. However, in order to be sure of their origin, I will be visiting the reservation and will talk to the tribal council. They will definitely identify the maker of this particular type of arrow."

Johnny slowly rose out of his chair. Two Mounties quickly blocked his path, but Sergeant Stewart motioned for them to move aside. Johnny slowly walked to the table. He reverently lifted one of the arrows, his hand shaking, as a single teardrop coursed down his cheek.

Belle, Jess, and Michelle came up behind Johnny.

Michelle placed her hand on Johnny's shoulder. Quietly she whispered, "What is it, Johnny?"

Johnny stared at the arrow. Slowly, his lips trembling, he raised his head. His eyes focussed in turn on Michelle, Belle, and Jess.

His voice was filled with grief as he haltingly

said, "It's…my dad's…arrow. Dad was out there helping me."

Belle in a solemn tone quietly said, "That's impossible, Darryl. Johnny's parents' belongings are in some boxes in our attic. Johnny was grief-stricken at the murder of his parents. When you and the other officers completed your investigation, you released all of Johnny's parents' belongings to him, but Johnny asked us to seal those things in boxes until he could bring himself to look at them. Those boxes have not been opened in the last four years."

"Belle, do you or Jess know which box holds Simon's rifle and archery equipment?"

"Yes. There's an itemized list of contents on each box."

Sergeant Stewart requested permission to retrieve the box from the attic. His footsteps could be heard echoing through the house as he went upstairs into the Gantry's attic. He returned carrying a large dust-covered box that he set on the front room floor. Carefully, he opened the box. He removed the contents placing them on the front room table. Then, he invited each person to examine the items. Darryl, his head bent in thought, slowly turned toward the others after they had returned to their seats.

"According to the records, there were six arrows in Simon's quiver at the time of the murders. Now, just one arrow remains in the quiver. Jess and I found the other five arrows. One was found in the tree by the stream and another was found sticking in a fence post on the property line. We located two arrows on the ground near Johnny's parents' house and one in the log near where you stood, Mr. Radonsky. We also found the three shotgun shells that you fired from your gun. We know Johnny couldn't have shot those arrows as he was hidden in his secret room behind the master bedroom closet."

Belle interrupted, "Darryl, who was the woman in the front room window that Jess saw while he was hiding in the woods? Obviously that's who Mr. Radonsky shot at!"

"I don't know, Belle. As Jess has confirmed, the figure looked like Lorelei, but nobody was there when we went inside. Johnny, do you have any idea who it might have been?"

"It was my mom. She was in the house protecting me."

Radonsky snorted, "I, for one, do not believe in ghosts. Obviously I didn't shoot anybody because there was nobody there!"

Sergeant Stewart's brow furrowed as he spoke, "For some reason, Mr. Radonsky, you appear to have been shooting with a Browning shotgun today. However, you usually shoot with an Ithaca, pump action, twelve gauge. It's funny how the mind works. Why you would switch back to your grandfather's gun is hard to understand. I'm sure that when we compare the shotgun shells that murdered Johnny's parents with what you were using today, we will find a direct match."

Radonsky suddenly looked defeated. He

stared at Johnny as he muttered; "My Ithaca has disappeared—probably stolen. I hope you understand, Johnny, that it was nothing personal. It was just that I saw your mom at all those parent-teacher meetings, but she would never even smile at me. She thought that she was better than me."

Darryl Stewart removed a piece of paper from his pocket.

"Four years ago, I found this paper lying in front of Johnny. Notice the design that you drew, Johnny. Where else have you seen that design today?"

"It's the same as the design on the stock of Mr. Radonsky's shotgun!"

"That's right, Johnny. I checked and I discovered that the initials in that design belonged to Stanley Radonsky, Mr. Radonsky's grandfather. Obviously the shotgun belonged to your grandfather, Mr. Radonsky. I understand that he was a respected guide of the Blackfoot tribe. Why you have chosen to hide your lineage when others, such as myself, celebrate our cultural inheritance is beyond me, but that, of course, is a matter best left to your own conscience."

Later, Sergeant Stewart put Radonsky in the back of one of his officers' squad cars. He stood watching, deep in thought as his men slowly drove out of the ranch yard and headed for Strathmore. The Sergeant returned to bid farewell to the Gantrys. He found Johnny standing with Belle and Jess beside him and the kids clustered all around them. They were watching the woods near the stream.

In the darkness of the woods, two *iridescent* figures raised their hands in farewell. A voice echoed through the woods, "We are so very proud of you, Johnny. All is well, little one. Remember us always. Now, we are going to our final resting place."

As Johnny watched, the figures slowly faded from sight. His voice choked with emotion as he cried out, "No, Mom and Dad, please don't leave me! I need you!"

Darryl Stewart turned to Johnny. Placing his hands on Johnny's shoulders, he said, "Don't be sad, Johnny. All is well for Lorelei and Simon. They are going home. Someday we will all join them, but for now, Belle, Jess, the kids, and I need you to be with us."

Then Sergeant Darryl Stewart smiled as he said, "Goodnight Belle, Jess, kids."

Belle followed him out to his squad car. Quietly she said, "Thank You, Darryl."

Fifteen minutes later, as solitary Darryl Stewart drove slowly down the dark country road toward the distant lights of Strathmore, he thought to himself, '*There are many questions left unanswered from this evening's events. But then again, as my Cherokee grandmother was fond of saying, it is best that some questions not be asked or answered.*'

* * *

Michelle extended her right hand to Johnny and said, “Let’s go for a walk. We need to talk.”

Belle grinned as she watched Johnny and Michelle walk hand in hand over to her and Jess’s favourite stream. Michelle sat down on a log, crossed her pretty legs and pulled Johnny down beside her. Her voice drifted up to the adults. It was very obvious that Michelle was doing all the talking and Johnny, very wisely, sat quietly listening.

Belle’s eyes glistened with deep affection as she smiled and held Jess’s hands.

“It appears that Johnny is learning what it means to be loved and cared for by someone special.”

“It seems to me that I got the same speech at about the same age as Johnny,” Jess reflected.

“Yes, you did. Johnny is a very lucky young man.”

THE PROTECTOR

Concealing myself behind Eric's legs, I timidly peeked at the ominous figure silhouetted in the front door entrance. Aunt Clara had come to visit! Giving me a scornful look, she entered the living room. She carefully laid her pillbox hat and cloth coat on the nearest easy chair. I retreated even further behind Eric's legs. Aunt Clara and I were *not* friends.

Suddenly, my eyes riveted on a small brown animal scurrying across the rug. An intruder had followed Aunt Clara into our home! Instantly, my hunter's instincts took over. I crouched, hissed and leaped at the unwelcome visitor. Unfortunately at that precise moment, Aunt Clara stepped forward to hug Eric. Much to my dismay, I finished my leap with all of my claws snarled in one of Aunt Clara's nylons.

Aunt Clara screamed in a tremulous voice, "Eric, get this crazy cat off my leg! She's scratching me!"

Aunt Clara's face had turned white as she stood there shaking. Then she began to vigorously shake her leg. The nylon ripped the length of her leg and I tumbled to the floor, still caught up in the nylon.

"Midnight! Let go!" Eric demanded.

I tried with all my might to disengage myself from the nylon, but my efforts created the opposite effect. I lay on my back completely tangled in the nylon, loudly howling in frustration and lashing my tail from side to side.

Eric, unable to keep a grin off his freckled face, loosened me claw by claw from the nylon and carefully lifted me off Aunt Clara's foot.

"I'm sorry, Aunt Clara," he said.

I quickly scrambled up his arm. Hiding behind his head, I timidly peeked at Aunt Clara who gave me a withering look with her icy-cold blue eyes.

At that moment, the back door slammed and Laura appeared covered with sweat and dressed in a burgundy jogging-suit. Her long blonde hair was in complete disarray. Entering the living room, she hurried toward Clara with her arms outstretched. Then she came to an abrupt halt and stared, open-mouthed, at her sister's legs.

Putting her hands in front of her mouth, Laura gasped, then quickly said to her sister, "Clara, what in heaven's name happened?"

"I'll tell you what happened! For no reason at all, this awful cat attacked me!"

"Oh, for crying out loud! I'm sorry, Clara. Why don't you go to Eric's bedroom and slip out of those nylons? I'll make a cold drink for all of us."

As Aunt Clara turned to leave the room, she stared up at Eric and me and said, "You have to do something about that cat. I hate to say it, but I think there's something seriously weird about Midnight."

Laura watched as her sister disappeared down the hall. Then she slowly turned toward Eric and me.

"Eric, I can't understand why Midnight attacked your Aunt."

"I don't know, Mom. One minute she was standing right here beside me, and then all of a sudden, she was flying through the air toward Aunt Clara. She's never done anything like that before."

"You know that Aunt Clara is nervous around cats. Let's just try to keep Midnight and your Aunt apart. Okay?"

"Yes, Mom."

Eric and I went into the kitchen.

Going into the master bathroom, Laura stripped out of her jogging suit, showered, and then tied her long hair into a bun. After she had finished cleaning up, she joined Eric and me in the kitchen where she laid out cold drinks and an angel food cake on the table. I leaped down from Eric's shoulder and sat primly beside him in the breakfast nook. Laura smiled at me as I stuck out my chest and began licking my front paws with my rough little tongue.

"Isn't she pretty, Eric? Just look at how her black fur glistens," Laura commented.

Aunt Clara returned from the bedroom wrapped in a terry-towel robe and sat in the nook directly across from me. She gave me an angry glance before she started to visit with Laura and Eric. I ignored those icy-blue eyes and sat enjoying the tidbits that Eric was secretly slipping me as he listened to the ladies visit.

Suddenly, my eyes riveted on the intruder. Appearing from thin air, he sat on the cushion behind Aunt Clara's shoulder. Staring around the room, his black nose quivering, the intruder stood motionless on his hind legs. I growled deep down in my throat. My body began to quiver as my tail lashed back and forth. The fur stood up on my back. Eric turned quickly, his large hands reaching for me, but it was too late, I had already sprung into the air toward the invader. I aimed my leap toward the back of the cushion beside Aunt Clara.

Aunt Clara's face turned white and she spat a white spray of angel food cake crumbs over the kitchen table as she screamed, "No, no, not again!"

Instead of staying out of my way, Aunt Clara unexpectedly moved into line with my leap, and then ducked. As I sailed over her head, my claws caught in her blonde hair.

The next thing I knew I was tumbling down behind Aunt Clara as she screamed, "My wig!"

When I came to a stop, I found that I was wedged between her and the back of the bench seat. Struggling with all of my might, I tried to untangle myself from Aunt Clara's hair, but my efforts again created the opposite effect. My claws were completely tangled in her wig. Again, I laid on my back howling in frustration.

Aunt Clara scrambled out of the breakfast nook. Her hands on her hips, she stood glaring down at me. "Eric, that cat is going to be the death of me! What on earth is wrong with her?"

Eric kneeled down beside the bench seat. He gently lifted me up and removed the wig. Gingerly, he handed the wig back to Aunt Clara who snatched it from him. Clara's usual Nordic fair-skinned facial features were a deep-red colour as she fled to the bedroom, sobbing. Laura, with an angry look on her face, took me from Eric and marched to the back landing. She put me down, walked back into the kitchen and firmly shut the basement door with a loud bang.

Scratching at the door, I howled in a pitiful tone for Eric to rescue me from my prison. I heard his plaintive voice, "Mom, it's not fair. Don't put Midnight downstairs. She *must* have seen something behind Aunt Clara that made her leap. Please don't put her downstairs, Mom."

"Eric, I didn't see anything and besides, as I already told you, we can't have Midnight attacking your Aunt. Midnight will be all right downstairs. She can come up at suppertime."

Later, lying on my mat, my ears perked up as I heard the sounds of supper being prepared. The basement door quietly opened revealing Eric's smiling face.

"Hi, Midnight! Mom says you can come back upstairs. Come on, jump up on my shoulder. That's my good girl."

When Eric and I went into the kitchen, Laura was hurrying around getting the food ready. Aunt Clara stood by the sink cleaning vegetables. She had repaired her hairdo and was smiling broadly as she gossiped with Laura. When she turned and noticed me, her icy-blue eyes gave me another cold look. Then she went back to work. Laura walked over to Eric and me. Reaching up, she gave me a gentle scratch behind one of my white-tufted ears. Then Eric placed me on one of the breakfast nook benches.

Laura leaned over to scratch my chest. "Now you little bandit, behave yourself. I don't want you jumping on Aunt Clara. You just lie here and be a good cat. Come on, Eric. You can set the table."

* * *

After supper, Aunt Clara and Eric decided to play a game of checkers. I stealthily crept through the house looking for my black-eyed enemy. Checking every nook and cranny, I conducted a thorough search. There was not a sign of the nuisance. I was sure that as an animal of the night, he had retired to some hiding place to sleep. Later that night, he would start prowling for food. In my mind, he was a constant threat to my human family. I was their protector and it was up to me to deal with this problem.

Laura paused from watching the game to look at me moving from room to room.

"Eric, what on earth is wrong with Midnight? She has been pacing through the house for the last hour. You don't suppose that she needs to go out?"

"I don't think so, Mom. I've already let her out. I don't know what's the matter with her."

"I guess Midnight is just restless. Eric, bring her to sit with us."

Eric picked me up and put me on the bench seat beside him.

Aunt Clara stared at me. Then she shook her head.

"Eric, I hate to say it, but I think cats are really kind of dumb animals. Midnight is pretty, but I'm sure she can't learn that much. I mean, you can't even teach her any tricks."

"Aunt Clara, I think Midnight is very clever. Midnight, get off the table! What are you doing? Look at that Aunt Clara, Midnight has made your move for you. You win!"

"Eric, Midnight was just lucky. Cats can't learn to play games."

Laura giggled. "Well, I don't know, big sister. It looks like Midnight helped you win!"

At bedtime, Eric went to sleep on the couch in the living room. When it was time for Clara and Laura to retire, Clara went to Eric's bedroom to settle in for the night. Propping herself up on a huge downy pillow, she started to read a mystery novel. She was, however, exhausted after a full day of travelling and visiting. Fifteen minutes later, she couldn't keep her eyes open. She groggily leaned over to turn out the nightstand light. Rolling over on her side, she was soon fast asleep.

Lying beside Eric on the couch in the living room, my ears twitched as I listened to the sounds of the house. The tapping sound of tiny claws on the main hallway's hardware floor echoed throughout the quiet house. Slowly I rose like a black panther on his nightly prowl and leaped quietly to the floor. I glided across the living room to the hallway entrance and peered around the corner. In the dimly-lit hall I saw a tiny animal slip through the open door of Eric's room. I crept stealthily to the doorway and into the bedroom. Standing, listening to Clara's breathing, I peered around the room.

Slowly, rising up out of the darkness, my tormentor appeared on the nightstand. I growled softly, the noise rumbling deep in my throat. I crouched, bunched my muscles, and then launched myself onto the nightstand. Landing, I was surprised to find him gone!

Then, I spotted my antagonist standing a few inches from Aunt Clara's face. Suddenly, Clara's eyes flew open and her breathing became laboured. Panic-stricken, she hugged her knees to her chest as she screamed, "Get away from me!"

Instantly the intruder skittered over to the dresser under the window.

I bounded across the bed and leaped. On the dresser Eric had several models of World War II planes and ships. The models went flying in all directions creating a loud crashing sound! But the little pest had turned and disappeared through the round opening in the window frame. A hand reached down in front of me and pushed down the little piece of wood that blocked the hole. Then, I was picked up and I found myself looking into

Eric's gentle eyes.

Eric smiled at me. "Way to go Midnight! I knew there must be some reason that you were leaping at Aunt Clara—you were trying to protect us from that mouse!"

Laura raced into the room. Her face had an expression of shock as she first looked at her sister, and then at Eric and his ruined models. Laura suddenly became aware of Clara's laboured breathing and immediately ran to her sister. Putting her arm around Clara, she began to comfort her. After a few moments had passed, Clara's breathing returned to normal.

"Its okay, Clara. This time Midnight has gone too far! I hate to do it, but while you're here, the cat is going to have to stay in the garage. Look what you've done, Midnight! You've scared the wits out of Aunt Clara, and you've ruined Eric's models. I love her, Eric, but I just can't have her acting this way."

"Mom, there was a mouse in the room! That's what scared Aunt Clara. Midnight was just trying to protect us."

"What? What are you talking about? A mouse in our house?"

"Yes, Mom. Midnight chased it and it zipped right out that hole in the window frame. Mom, it's the truth."

Aunt Clara looked at me with tears in her eyes. Those eyes no longer looked icy-cold, but were filled with relief. In a barely audible voice she whispered, "Laura, it's true. I woke up and there was a mouse looking right at me! Midnight chased it right out of here. I guess all this time she's been trying to protect us."

Leaping down out of Eric's arms, I stuck my tail in the air and then marched out of the room without a glance at Aunt Clara. Clara looked at Eric and Laura.

Laura grinned as she watched me go. "It's okay, Clara. Cats are very independent. Midnight will make up to you in her own time. Let's go down to the living room and I will make us some tea. We need to settle down after all this excitement."

An hour later, Laura sat on the floor of the living room in front of a roaring fire talking to Eric and Clara. I wandered into the room and lay behind Eric.

Clara quietly said to Laura, "I would really love to be friends with Midnight, but you know I've been afraid of cats since that incident on Uncle Harold's farm."

A tear rolled down Aunt Clara's cheek as she cast a glance at me out of the corners of her eyes.

Laura hugged her sister and kissed her firmly on the cheek.

"Nobody could have guessed that that old farm cat would attack and bite you, Clara. Maybe after all these years, it's time to take a chance. Midnight is a very special loving cat, and I think her pride was hurt because of the way we reacted to her antics. Maybe the way to start is by simply giving her an apology."

Across the room, I warily watched Aunt Clara's every move.

"I'm sorry, Midnight, I didn't realize you were trying to protect me. Cats frighten me and make me very nervous. I would like it if we could try and be friends."

Aunt Clara slowly held out her hands toward me.

I stared at her for a long time. My tail slowly moved from side to side. Eric looked down at me, scratched my ears and grinned. Slowly, I walked over to Aunt Clara, my tail sticking up in the air. I sat down directly in front of her, placed my paw on her leg and looked deeply into her eyes. Aunt Clara smiled. Tears rolled down her cheeks. Then, she reached down to scratch my ears … and I purred!

THE CHANCE MEETING

Thea sat alone at a table near the edge of the airport's busy food court and gazed down onto the Departures Level. Her eyes followed a solitary man's every move. She was aware only of him; all else was totally dismissed. Her face was a stoical mask betraying none of her inner thoughts or emotions. The man, broad-shouldered and with a lean, athletic build, was wearing black dress pants, a leather bombardier jacket and an emerald-coloured golf shirt. Gradually dwindling from her sight he moved slowly, but inexorably toward the doors that would give him access into Concourse A. She was painfully aware that in a scant few moments he would pass through security and on toward the plane, Dominion Air Flight 649 to Regina, departing from her life forever. Suddenly, Thea leaned her head into the palms of her hands. Tears burst forth from her eyes and her shoulders shook.

She thought to herself, '*Oh, Trent, you have touched my heart. For the briefest moment you rekindled my desire to love and be loved, but now you are gone because I was fearful to open the door that our chance meeting offered us. I have nothing left, but emptiness. Nothing to remind me of the love that might have been.'*

* * *

Thea Tipton, Stock Officer for Dominion Air Calgary Based Operations, sat at her double pedestal mahogany desk staring out of the window as her mind wandered back over events of the past three years. Tears slowly coursed down her cheeks eventually falling on her deep-blue, cashmere sweater that matched the colour of her eyes. Her thoughts centred on the saddest chapter of her thirty-three years when her beloved husband, Phil, a pilot and a minority owner of Dominion Air, had been involved in an airplane crash. In attempting to land his Boeing 747-300SF Transport on a small South Seas Island, Second World War vintage airstrip, while bringing free supplies donated by the airline to a missionary's medical clinic, he had been tragically killed when an engine malfunctioned.

During the first few weeks after his death, Thea's time had revolved around funeral arrangements, providing strength to her twin teenage girls, Caylen and Caitlin, and privately grieving the loss of her husband. To add to her troubles, she had soon discovered that her lawyers were more interested in prolonging the settlement of Phil's estate and draining funds into their own coffers, rather than acting in good faith on behalf of her and her daughters. Thea had petitioned the courts and forced the unscrupulous lawyers to appear in front of a judge. There she had confidently stood up, opened her file folder, and proceeded assertively to point out a number of questionable moves authored by the lawyers in the handling of her husband's estate. In the end, the judge awarded Thea a huge cash settlement plus court costs that she later invested for the future of Caylen and Caitlin.

Thea had worked in the front office in a variety of administration positions for Dominion Airlines throughout her marriage. When Phil was killed, she had taken a leave of absence not only for herself, but also for the girls. On the completion of her court settlement, she had left a telephone message for Brock Cornell, a family friend, mentor, and the majority owner of Dominion Air, informing him that she was ready to return to work.

However, plans were astir that would take Thea's life in a new direction. She recalled that early the next morning she had received a call from Brock. He had asked her to meet him the following day at the airport for lunch in Dominion Air's executive lounge. That afternoon having finished a lengthy lunch, Brock and Thea had sat silently lingering over their expresso coffees for several minutes staring out of the window overlooking the airport's runways. Out on the approach to the east-west runway huge commercial jets had lined up, waiting their turn to take off, their powerful engines filling the air with thunderous shrieks that rattled the windows of the terminal.

Brock's deep gravelly voice had penetrated the din as he had started to speak. "Thea, what would you think of transferring to Calgary to assume the position of Stock Officer?"

Thea remembered thinking to herself for a minute then after she had smoothed an errant blonde lock of hair out of her eyes she had replied to Brock's question. "It's a wonderful opportunity, Brock, but why me? You have far more experienced people to fill that position and besides I have two energetic thirteen-year-old daughters to consider. Though I'm egotistical enough to think that I'm quite capable of handling the position, I would have to work with a lot of experienced men and women who I'm afraid would not be very accepting of having a woman for a boss. Do I look like a tough Stock Officer to you?"

"You're worried about what people see on the surface, but I know what you have to offer on the inside. You have a rare combination of brains, toughness, abilities, and talents." Brock had then leaned back in his chair and stroked his beard as he blew smoke rings to the ceiling from his fat Havana cigar. "For gosh sakes, Thea, I've thrust you into more positions around here than any other person. Time and time again you've dug in and done a great job. Plus, look at the way you handled those shysters over Phil's estate."

Thea had smiled to herself as she remembered that Brock had paused, blown another smoke ring, and then looked out of the window to stare at a Dominion Air Boeing 747 300-SF Transport.

He had then turned back toward Thea. His eyes were sad, as he had slowly picked up his drink.

"To Phil, the best friend, pilot, father, husband, and partner that ever lived. May he rest in peace."

Thea had smiled sadly then had slowly raised her drink and gently touched Brock's glass. "I miss him so much, Brock. Not a day goes by that I don't think of my darling Phil. The evenings after the girls are safely tucked in bed are the hardest and the most lonely because then I'm alone with nothing, but my memories. When does it stop, Brock? When do you stop feeling so lonesome and empty? I'll be strong for my daughters—they need me to be a mother. They don't need to lose another parent. I've cried many tears for Phil, but may the Lord forgive me, I've also cried for myself."

Brock had stared into Thea's grief-filled eyes then reached across the table with his right hand and covered her hands. Thea and Brock turned again to stare out of the window. The Boeing 747-300SF Transport was rolling down the runway picking up speed then it majestically lifted off into the air. The two friends said nothing as they sat watching the plane disappear from sight.

"Thea, the time is right personally and professionally for you to move up to a head administrative position in the company. The Calgary operation has great personnel, but they need somebody with drive and leadership qualities. Somebody who is firm and can lead them into becoming a team."

Thea's lips had slowly broadened into a smile. "Brock, I want to thank you for the compliments, but I still have some reservations."

Brock had leaned forward tapping his cigar

on the ashtray. "You're welcome. I'll need you in the new position in one month."

"One month!"

"Yes."

"Brock, I need a bit of time to discuss your proposal with Caitlin and Caylen. After all the move would be disruptive to their social and academic lives."

"Okay. Talk it over with the girls tonight. I would really like to have your answer by tomorrow morning."

* * *

Thea sighed audibly in the silence of her office as she remembered curling up on her king-sized bed in her warm cuddly duvet with her girls. She had taken a deep breath and then told them about Brock's job offer. Tears had flooded out of Caitlin and Caylen's eyes as they realized that they would be leaving their friends and school.

"Girls, don't forget that your grandparents live in Calgary," Thea had gently reminded them.

As the twins had dried their tears, they had looked at each other and mischievous smiles had slowly broken out on their angelic faces. Caitlin had then nestled her head onto one of Thea's shoulders.

"Gee, Mom, going to grandma and grandpa's house will be a lot more fun than having to report to the neighbours. Caylen and I think that you should take the position." Caitlin had winked at her sister. "Right, Caylen!"

Caylen had snuggled up onto Thea's other shoulder as she exclaimed, "Sounds great to me!"

Thea thought about how the next morning she had approached Brock's office after a long restless night and quietly rapped on his open door.

Brock, who was talking on his telephone, had put his hand over the receiver and then had called out, "Come on in, Thea."

Thea had walked into his executive office and sat down in front of his dark mahogany desk. Sitting on the cadenza in Brock's office were models of the airplanes that the company flew ranging from the Boeing 727 to the 747. Her eyes focussed on the 747 and she thought of Phil. Brock who had finished talking on the telephone watched her for a few minutes and then leaned forward in his chair.

"Morning, Thea, and may I say that you look terrible? Didn't you get any sleep last night?"

"Morning, Brock. No, I don't think I slept at all. Thea shifted her eyes from the model of the 747 to look at Brock. She grinned and said, "Thanks for the compliment."

Brock had laughed. "You're welcome!"

"Okay, Brock, I've thought about the job offer. I guess we can get organized and be in Calgary by the end of the month. The girls and I have agreed that the move will be good because my parents live there and *it is* a great opportunity to advance my career. They assured me that grandma and grandpa would love to have them over. Those two scamps probably figure that going to my parents' house means no rules and therefore it will be nothing be fun."

Brock had grinned, looked up at the ceiling, shaken his head, and then given a short snorting laugh.

"Thea, I've known your mom and dad for years. What the heck, your dad and I started this airline by flying charters for the tourists looking for sun and fun. With an awful lot of hard work we managed to make Dominion Air what it is today. I just wish your dad hadn't left the airline to build those futuristic hybrid engines, but I guess that was always his first love. Anyway, I think Caitlin and Caylen will find that Joyce and George have the same high expectations for them as they had for you. I know how close you are to them and I hoped you would jump at the chance to be near them. Don't worry, the company will help you find a place to live in Calgary while we assist you in selling your condominium here. Thea, look upon this move as a new start to your life. Perhaps you will meet somebody interesting. You are still a young, intelligent, beautiful woman. Don't make the mistake that I did and immerse yourself in work to the exclusion of all else. It's time to get on with your life."

Thea remembered that she had shaken her head vigorously and then looked up at Brock as she had softly spoken. "Brock, I'm not interested in meeting anyone else. Phil was the one true love of my life. I was eighteen years old when I was lucky enough to meet him. It was just one of those unexplainable chance meetings. I had finished my classes for the day at the university and had gone to the Abbottsford Airport to pick up dad who was flying in from Calgary. There was Phil out on the tarmac working on his vintage Spitfire in his favourite, old, faded coveralls that were covered with grease, sweat and dirt. He was filthy, but when he looked at me with those dark brown eyes, I made a fool of myself and practically begged him to have supper with me just like a silly boy- crazy teenage girl. I was scared stiff that he would say no or maybe laugh at me, but he just gave me one of his great dazzling smiles and said yes.

After we had been dating for only a month, I almost gave mom and dad heart attacks when I informed them that Phil and I were going to get married. A month later, thanks to their help, the deed was done. Two years later the girls were born. I have had twelve years of happiness with him to remember. No, I will be happy to help my girls get through their teenage years, get spoiled by my parents, and make the operation in Calgary run smoothly. Romantic entanglements are definitely a thing of the past for me."

Thea smiled to herself as she recalled how Brock had turned his head back toward the window and a mischievous smile had appeared on his lips. Thea had grinned back at him, "What are you thinking, Brock?"

Brock had said, "I'm thinking that a new job brings with it fresh opportunities. I love you dearly. You are the daughter that I never had. Take the job because you are the best, but also because it is time for you to move on with your life. Perhaps, who knows, despite what you think maybe some handsome guy will appear to sweep you off your feet."

* * *

Thea leaned forward in her office and picked up Phil's picture. She held the picture to her chest as she whispered, "Bless you, Brock, for all your support and kindness, but you were wrong. I am happy with the opportunity that you have given me and I am at peace. It is enough for me to live the rest of my life with my memories of Phil. No man will ever capture my heart again."

* * *

"Ladies and gentlemen, this is Captain Rogers. We are reducing our altitude and cruising speed. In fifteen minutes we will be making an unscheduled landing at the Calgary International Airport. There is no need for concern. One of the warning lights on our instrument panel is malfunctioning, and, as a precaution and in order to ensure the safety of you the passengers, we will be making a brief stop in Calgary. I repeat, there is no need for concern."

A persistent buzzing noise suddenly disrupted the stillness in Thea's office. Her thoughts were brought to an abrupt halt as she slowly picked up the telephone receiver.

As Dominion Air Flight 649 was beginning its final approach to the Calgary Airport, Trent Krause was deep in thought as he stroked his clean-shaven chin and stared out of the window of the sleek Boeing 727. He was totally unaware of the flashing sign above his head repeatedly reminding him to fasten his seat belt. Even the soft, but authoritative voice of the head flight attendant that permeated the interior of the airplane reminding the passengers to fasten their seat belts didn't rouse him from his reverie. Finally, a flight attendant got Trent's attention when she leaned over, gently touched his arm and pointed down at his seat belt. He grinned back and cinched up the belt.

Trent turned back to peer out of the window as he pondered an e-mail that he had received on his laptop computer from Keira, his administrative assistant. Two weeks ago, Trent had purchased the controlling shares in a farm implement business based in Regina that had fallen on hard times due mostly to its inefficient collection of outstanding accounts. When he had made an offer to purchase, the stockholders who held 51% of the stock had quickly voted to accept much to the chagrin of the president, Tory Robinson.

Despite making several phone calls to Tory to arrange a meeting with him at Abbottsford where Trent's company headquarters were located, Keira had reported to him that Tory had always found an excuse not to come to a meeting. Finally, Trent decided that enough was enough. Thinking it wise to meet on Tory's home turf, he had made arrangements to fly to Regina. Before leaving, he had instructed Keira to send an e-mail to Tory to advise him that he was coming. Tory had responded with a pointed e-mail of his own indicating that he would meet with Trent, but he would use every legal move possible to block him. Keira had forwarded Tory's e-mail to Trent on the airplane.

Trent sat staring out of the window of the airplane, shaking his head as he thought about Tory. He knew Tory had built his farm implement business from nothing and obviously must have great strengths, but something had gone wrong. He had hoped to avoid a confrontation and to work with Tory in setting things right, but he guessed things just simply couldn't be done from a point of harmony.

Passengers tend to sit quietly, almost apprehensively, when an airplane makes its final landing approach to a runway. It's almost as if they are waiting to re-establish a connection with Mother Earth. They are coming back home to their natural element.

Suddenly, an elderly man yelled yanking Trent out of his reverie and completely disrupting the stillness of the airplane.

"My wife! There's something wrong with my wife! For God's sake, she's not breathing!"

Trent looked across the aisle to see an elderly lady slumped over. Only her seat belt kept her from completely collapsing into the aisle. Quickly he released his seat belt and knelt in front of the lady. He felt for her pulse then released her seat belt, laid her down in the aisle, and began to give her cardiopulmonary respiration. Mere seconds had past when the flight attendant who had reminded him about his seatbelt appeared at his shoulder.

"Sir, I can take over now."

Trent shook his head quietly muttering, "I don't want to stop. I'll lose the rhythm of the chest compressions and breathing."

In a few moments, the elderly woman started to breathe on her own. Trent with the flight attendant's assistance lifted the woman up and gently placed her in her seat. The plane lurched as it touched the ground throwing Trent backward onto the seats behind him. The flight attendant fell backward on top of Trent causing her skirt to ride high up on her hips. A couple of flight attendants, who couldn't help, but giggle, quickly rushed forward and helped her. Blushing, she quickly smoothed her short skirt down to its proper position, but not before Trent caught a fleeting glimpse of her long, shapely legs.

Also blushing, Trent moved back to his seat and sat down. He quickly turned to look out of the window as the airplane slowly approached and nuzzled up to its gate. Turning his head, he was surprised to see the young flight attendant looking down at him, her soft brown eyes gazing intently at him.

"Hi! My name's Joan. Mr. Simpson and I wish to thank you for your assistance with his wife. Perhaps you would let me treat you to a soft drink or coffee on behalf of Dominion Air." Joan's lovely lips broadened into a smile. "I hope you don't consider me to be too forward."

"Hi! I'm Trent Krause. I don't consider you too forward, but I'm sorry I must reluctantly decline your kind offer. I have an agenda to prepare for a meeting in Regina, but thank you for the invitation."

At that moment the front door of the airplane opened and the flight attendants took their positions to assist the passengers in disembarking. As the passengers exited out through Gate A16 into Concourse A, they were directed by Dominion Air representatives to sit in the waiting area. They were instructed not to leave the terminal; however, they were free to mill about the airport. As soon as the problem was corrected an announcement over the loud speaker would inform them to return to the concourse. Captain Rogers and his crew assembled near the check-in counter. Ground crews could be seen through the concourse windows rapidly removing the starboard engine cowling.

As Trent sat looking around, his eyes focussed on a tall female figure moving quickly toward him down the concourse. He stared at the blonde-haired woman dressed in a Dominion Air blue blazer, a pastel blue cashmere sweater and matching skirt. Watching with deep interest, he noticed Captain Rogers hustling over to meet her. The woman's deep blue eyes looked in his direction and locked with his. She smiled then quickly turned back to give her attention to the Captain's report, but every so often she would steal a glance in his direction. Feeling a bit embarrassed, Trent found that he couldn't seem to take his eyes off her and he felt a strong desire to know her.

Then he thought, *'Trent, don't be silly! You don't just look at somebody and decide that you want to be with her. That kind of stuff is for teenagers whose hormones are out of whack and for Romance Novels, not for boring thirty-three-year-old businessmen. Besides, I wouldn't stand a chance with that gorgeous woman. Anyway, I'm just too busy for women. I guess she must be somebody important considering how Captain Rogers and his crew are hovering around her.'*

The crew and the woman finished talking. Joan pointed her finger at Trent and the blonde beauty looked in his direction. The woman immediately started walking toward him. For some reason Trent felt like a very small boy as he suddenly developed an inexplicable panicky desire to run away down the concourse. He watched as the woman glided nearer. His hands started to sweat and he deliberately averted his eyes toward the windows. Chills ran up Trent's back as a low, soft voice started to speak.

"Hello. My name is Thea Tipton. I'm the Stock Officer for Dominion Air."

Trent forced himself to look up into Thea's eyes. He stood quickly and shook hands with her.

"Hello. I'm Trent Krause. It's a pleasure meeting you, Ms. Tipton."

"Please, just call me Thea."

"Okay, if you will call me Trent."

"Trent, I want to thank you for helping Mrs. Simpson."

"Oh, it was nothing. I'm sure that anyone would have done the same thing."

Thea smiled and shook her head.

"Actually I don't think many people would have done what you did. People have a tendency in this day and age not to get involved. I'm surprised that Joan didn't notice that Mrs. Simpson was in distress when she checked the passengers prior to landing. I will have to speak to her and brush her up a little bit on her observational skills. Passengers shouldn't be doing a flight attendant's job."

Trent looked into Thea's eyes and vigorously shook his head.

"Ms. Tipton, Thea, with all due respect, the flight attendant didn't initially have an opportunity to deal with the problem because I was right across the aisle from Mrs. Simpson and also Mrs. Simpson's problem happened after Joan had checked the passengers for landing. I don't think it was possible for her to react any faster. A few moments after I had started CPR, she was beside me to give assistance. Thea, I am going to write a letter of commendation for her personnel file. I think she and the other flight attendants did a great job."

Thea thought to herself, *'Oh, my God! Trent reminds me so much of my Phil. Phil was always so passionate in giving credit to those who deserved it and he would go to the greatest lengths to make sure the company recorded special actions by the crews in their personnel files. What a handsome-looking man and so kind. My heart is pounding so hard I'm afraid that he's going to hear it. This man is just so special. Thea, get control of yourself! You don't even know him! Let's get on with doing our job.'*

"It's my responsibility to investigate all aspects of every incident especially ones that jeopardize the lives of the passengers and crew members. Joan's record as a flight attendant is exemplary and I'm sure that she would be most appreciative if you would write a letter on her behalf. I will make sure that the original is placed in her personnel file and that she gets a copy."

"I noticed that there are some computer terminals against the wall. If you will give me your e-mail address, I will write a letter for Joan on my laptop and forward it on to you. I might as well do it now because I'm not going anywhere until the plane is fixed, and besides, I have a short agenda to prepare for my meeting in Regina." Suddenly Trent stopped talking. He stood quietly for a few minutes looking deep into Thea's eyes. Time seemed to stop. Then Trent asked hesitantly, "Perhaps you would like to have coffee with me after I'm done."

Thea answered a bit breathlessly, "I'd love to go with you, but as Stock Officer I'm afraid I have to stay here and keep an eye on the repairs to the airplane."

"Can't you have your assistant or somebody else supervise until we get back."

"No. Oh, Trent, I really want to have coffee

with you, but I can't."

"I guess it's no different than me going to Regina to meet good old Tory Robinson. Can't really pass the job on to someone else. I have to do it myself."

Finding herself reluctant to leave, Thea asked, "Who's Tory Robinson?"

"He's the president of a farm implement company in Regina. I just managed to buy the controlling stock in his company a couple of weeks back. Tory utterly refuses to meet me in Abbotts-ford, so I'm flying out there to meet him on his home turf. I really hope that Tory and I can break the ice. I mean, all I want to do is sort out why he has so many outstanding accounts. It seems to be the main reason that his stockholders bailed out on him."

"I'm sure that you will find a way." Although Thea knew her duties called her elsewhere, she felt so drawn to Trent that she began babbling on, "It's a good bet that most of those outstanding accounts are owed the company by the local farmers. I know the Saskatchewan farmers in general have had a rough few years and several companies have given them extended lines of credit, but now things seem to be turning around. My dad told me once that he remembered the farmers coming to Regina after they had sold their crops. They visited all the businesses that they owed money to and paid all their bills. In fact, it's not too dissimilar to the airline business where we can have two quarters of losses and a couple where we make huge profits.

As long as the profits outweigh the losses things will be fine. Perhaps Tory just has to know that you want to understand the nature of his business, and then he will become more cooperative."

Suddenly a booming voice overrode their discussion. "You'd better listen to this young lady." Brock stood behind Thea smiling broadly.

Thea whirled around and wrapped her arms around Brock. Then she quickly stepped back with an embarrassed look on her face and glanced at Trent.

"Brock, where the heck did you come from?"

"Well, you know that charter that you have going to Las Vegas?"

"Yes."

"It appeared that the crew was here, but the designated plane for that trip was delayed by some repairs in our hangar in Vancouver. So I grabbed myself a pilot for the second chair and decided to fly it out here. Besides, it's been ages since I saw your folks and your girls."

Trent's face visibly paled. He thought to himself, '*After all these years I finally find someone that I could care about and she's married.*'

Brock paused for a moment. His eyes swept the waiting area taking in the passengers sitting waiting then he focussed on Trent and Thea. Extending his hand to Trent he said, "Hi. My name is Brock Cornell."

Gripping Brock's hand firmly in his Trent replied, "Nice to meet you, Brock. I'm Trent

Krause. You must be one of the pilots that fly for Thea. Strikes me that you're lucky to have her as your boss."

Thea laughed as she shook her head. "Brock is the owner of Dominion Air, my boss, and a close friend of my family, Trent. He and my dad flew together in the military and commercially. In fact, my dad and Brock started Dominion Air back in the stone age when they had to wind up the propellers to make the planes fly." Thea gave Brock an impish smile and continued. "Brock, Trent assisted a lady passenger, a Mrs. Simpson, on Flight 649 who for some unknown reason had stopped breathing. I think the airline owes him a big thank you for helping us out."

"I'll have you know, young lady, that back in the Stone Age we really flew airplanes and didn't depend on some computer to do our jobs for us!" Brock smiled back at Thea and winked at her then turned to look at Trent. "Anyway, Trent, I want to thank you on behalf of the airline." Looking from one to the other Brock quickly added, "Thea, I think you and I should treat Trent to coffee and pie. By the way, Thea, why is Flight 649 here in Calgary?"

"Brock, I can't leave here. Flight 649's instruments were indicating a malfunction in the starboard engine. I had better stay here to supervise any needed repairs. Anyway, Trent has told me that he has to type out an agenda for a business meeting that he has in Regina and he wants to write a letter of commendation for Joan, one of our flight attendants." Thea stood staring into Trent's eyes. "Perhaps Trent and I can slip away after the plane is fixed and he has his work done," Thea added.

Brock shook his head then smiled while patting Trent on the shoulder. "Thea, you'd better get yourself out to that plane and light a flame under those glorified mechanics. In the meantime, I'll take the crew and Trent down to the Food Fair for a hot cup of coffee and a big piece of pie. Come join us when things are finished here."

Trent seeing his chances of being alone with Thea slipping away muttered, "But I need to..." He thought, '*Oh, my God. I can't let this woman walk out of my life.*'

Brock immediately broke in. "Trent, our planes are equipped with computer plug-ins so you can use your laptop on the flight to Regina and easily get your work done. I'll give you our e-mail address and you can send Joan's letter back to us. Now, let's go get the crew and be on our way."

Thea's eyes quickly looked away as if afraid he would be able to read there the longing to be with him, if only for a little while. Her blue eyes went icy as she shifted her eyes to glare angrily at Brock.

"Perhaps Trent should go ahead with you, Brock, but I was hoping to treat him to coffee myself. After all, I am the Stock Officer of the Calgary operations and it would seem only right that I treat Trent on behalf of the airline." '*Why am I so angry at Brock*?' Thea wondered to herself.

Brock, seemingly unfazed by Thea's angry

look, ignored her comment and firmly said, “Thea, we’ll see you down at the Food Fair.” He planted a hand behind Trent’s back and firmly propelled him forward. “Come on, Trent, let’s collect the crew and get going. Coffee and pie are awaiting us.”

Trent glanced over at Thea as Brock guided him over to the reception area. She sighed deeply, shook her head, looked away from the two men, and walked across the concourse to talk to a couple of passengers.

As the two men walked over to the flight deck crew and the flight attendants, Thea looked at them out of the corners of her eyes. Brock spoke to the crew, gestured in the direction of the Food Fair, and then the entire group walked away from Thea on down the concourse. As she watched them disappearing into the distance, she noticed that Joan made a special effort to walk beside Trent. Thea could hear Joan’s hearty laugh as she chattered with him. Every few minutes Joan would smooth back her hair as she smiled up at Trent.

‘Oh fine,’ thought Thea, *‘I meet a man who for the first time in three years I would like to know a little bit better, at least have a chance to share coffee with him, and this happens. Thanks a lot, Brock. I love you like my own sweet dad, but right now I think you’re a rat! And that goes for you too, Joan!’*

Thea suddenly realized that somebody was speaking to her when a large calloused hand gently touched her arm.

“Ms. Tipton, I’m sorry to interrupt, but I

thought you'd like to see the findings on Flight 649."

Thea stared blankly at Rick, her chief technician, for a few long minutes.

"I'm sorry, Rick. I didn't hear you."

"The findings on Flight 649. We've completed our analysis, Ms. Tipton."

"That's great, Rick. What did you find?"

"We can find nothing wrong with the starboard engine, but we did find a malfunction in a component of the instrument panel which we have corrected."

Although Thea's facial expression was completely devoid of emotion, she quickly praised Rick by saying, "Great work, Rick. Tell your crew that I'm really impressed with their efficiency. I guess we can go ahead and embark the passengers. Let's get them on their way. We've held them up long enough."

Rick slowly ran his fingers through his tousled hair and then shook his head. "Ms. Tipton, with your permission I would like my guys to repeat their tests. Also, I would like Captain Rogers and his crewmembers to run some checks of their own before they leave us. I just want to be sure that everything is okay."

Thea thought for a moment. A smile lit up her face. She nodded at Rick. "Okay, Rick. I'll go down to the Food Fair and send the flight deck crew back to join you."

She thought to herself, *'Maybe I can figure out something subtle to say to Brock to get him to leave Trent and me alone. Oh, Thea, what's the matter with you? Why are you scheming to be alone with Trent? What's happening to you?'*

As Thea walked briskly down the concourse, her mind was filled with ideas all pointed toward removing Brock Cornell from the Food Fair and leaving her alone with Trent. But by the time she had reached the base of the escalator that would take her up to the Food Fair, she had still not come up with anything. The problem was that Brock Cornell did not react well to subtle suggestions. He was the type of man who saw the world in black and white, not subtle gray.

Mounting the escalator, she decided that the best plan was to take Brock aside and tell him bluntly to leave. Screwing up her courage, she stepped off the escalator and walked toward Brock, Trent, and the others.

Suddenly, Thea heard her mother's voice cry out, "Thea, honey, we're here!"

"Two identical teenage ponytailed girls dressed in identical red tank tops and hip hugging jeans shouted, "Hey, Mom!"

Thea turned to see her mom, dad, and daughters entering the Food Fair from the escalator opposite her. Her dad immediately saw Brock and rushed over to him to shake hands. Her mom and the girls gave her some big hugs.

Thea shook her head as she said, "Mom, what's everybody doing here?"

Joyce shook her head in wonderment as she laughed, "I suppose you've been so busy that you forgot you invited us for supper. By the way, you *did* say that you were paying!"

Thea bent her head, covered her eyes with her hand, and shook her head.

"Sorry, Mom, we had the Regina flight from Vancouver develop some problems, so I've been busy supervising the repairs and taking care of the passengers. I completely forgot about supper."

Joyce took Thea's hands in her own. "It's okay, dear. We're here now, so let's eat. Taking Thea's arm Joyce turned and walked over to the table to join her husband and the others.

"Who is this handsome gentleman?"

Thea looked across the table at Trent whose eyes locked with hers while he patiently listened to Brock and George reminisce about the old times.

"Mom, I'd like to introduce you to Trent Krause. Trent assisted an elderly lady passenger who stopped breathing on Flight 649. Brock and I decided to treat him to coffee and pie."

Joyce's blue eyes studied Thea and Trent. She noticed how intently they stared at each other and the wisp of a smile briefly graced her facial features then just as quickly it was gone.

"How do you do, Trent. My name is Joyce Williamson and of course you have already met my husband, George. These blonde-haired dynamos are our granddaughters, Thea's daughters, Caitlin and Caylen Tipton.

The twin blonde teenagers studied Trent for a few moments, glanced at each other, then said, "Hi!"

"It's nice to meet you, Mrs. Williamson, Caitlin, Caylen."

Glancing at Thea who had sat down quietly at the table, Trent offered his hand to Joyce and the girls. The girls giggled and then shook Trent's hand.

Thea turned to look at Captain Rogers and said, "Captain, Rick would like you and your crew to return to the aircraft. He wants you and the flight deck crew to run some tests. The flight attendants can get things ready in the aircraft for departure." Joan's mouth opened as if she were going to make a comment, but then she rose from her seat without saying a word and started to walk toward Concourse A.

Captain Rogers watched Joan leave then grinned as he spoke, "Trent, it was an honour and a real pleasure meeting you. Thanks again for helping us out with Mrs. Simpson. Okay, crew, let's get back to work."

"It was a pleasure meeting you too, Captain Rogers."

The Captain and his crew departed in a group to walk back to the airplane. Thea watched Joan as she waited by the escalator for the others to catch up with her. The entire group then rode down the escalator, walked toward the doors to Concourse A, and disappeared as they moved beyond the sliding doors into the concourse.

"I guess I'm not too popular with some people," muttered Thea.

Joyce leaned sideways in her chair as she

whispered into Thea's ear, "Seems like somebody has eyes only for you, Thea."

Just then Caitlin's voice took on an angry tone as she interrupted her grandma, "Mom, Caylen and I are having a very serious disagreement with Grandma Joyce. It's really important that you hear our side of the problem and tell grandma how unfair she's being."

"Yes, it's really serious," exclaimed Caylen.

Caitlin and Caylen crossed their arms and looked defiantly at their grandma who looked back at them, her face devoid of all expression.

"Yes, Mom, continued Caylen. "We want you to tell grandma that our new outfits will be great for our dance number in the festival at the Jubilee Auditorium. Grandma says that they are completely and utterly unacceptable. She says they're too skimpy!"

With a flourish the twin girls reached into some bags and laid their dance costumes on the table then looked expectantly at their mother. The men immediately stopped talking and looked at the women. Thea's cheeks turned red and her eyes took on a steely shade.

"Girls, where on earth did you get these outfits?"

"Mrs. Witherall at the Black Cat Dress Shop said we could show them to you, Mom," said Caitlin.

"Well, Mrs. Witherall sells merchandise to adult women and also specializes in outfits for professional performers. What were the two of you doing in that store?"

The two girls smoothed back their hair, looked at each other, fidgeted in their seats, and then looked down at their hands. Caitlin glanced nervously up at Thea.

"Mom, Mrs. Witherall said we have the figures of grown-up women now and can wear these," firmly stated Caitlin. "I mean some of our things have to be adult-sized because, well, you know."

"The answer is NO! These outfits are too revealing. You are two thirteen-year-old teenage girls. You're too young to wear such outfits," Thea firmly stated.

"Sure, Mom, you would take grandma's side. It figures." Caitlin groaned as she stared angrily down at the table.

"Caitlin and Caylen, you heard what your mother said. Now the matter is closed," Joyce stated firmly.

"And it figures that you would take mom's side," Caylen muttered.

"Caylen and Caitlin! Enough is enough!" Thea's voice rose in pitch and volume as it took on an ominous cutting tone.

George and Brock sat listening to the exchange wisely choosing not to interfere, but Trent slowly and cautiously started to speak, "Thea, if it would be all right... May I give my opinion as a professional businessman as well as an interested outside observer? I know I'm not a member of your family and I'm probably speaking out-of-turn, but I think I may have a way to resolve this problem. Of course, the final decision is without question yours."

George, Brock, and Joyce looked at each other and exchanged meaningful glances.

"Trent is a brave man," George whispered quietly to Brock.

Brock nodded his head and whispered back, "I wish him the best of luck. He has stuck his head into the middle of something that could cost him that rugged handsome head. You don't get between a mother and her teenage daughters. Right, George?"

"Right, Brock. It's kind of like getting between a mother grizzly and her cubs."

"Shush you two," whispered Joyce.

Everybody sat in stony silence as Thea sat staring at Trent for a very long time then slowly in measured tones she said, "All right, Trent, what is your opinion?"

Trent leaned over and withdrew a couple of softcovered, glossy, coil-bound books from his briefcase.

"Caitlin and Caylen, these books are two copies of a description of my company and all our holdings." He handed each girl a copy. "On the first page you will see pictures of the chief executive company officers."

"Who's this woman? She's beautiful!" exclaimed Caitlin.

"Girls, that is my chief administrative assistant, Keira, an extremely attractive lady who looks equally good in fashionable or in casual clothes. However, she always wears blazers, elegant sweaters, slacks, and skirts around the office." Trent gestured with his right hand at Thea. "In fact, she dresses very much like your mom. Why is that?"

Caitlin laughed. "That's easy! She's trying to dress well because that's what's expected in your business. But Mr. Krause, my sister and I are dancing in a festival. It's different!"

"Is it? Doesn't the organization that runs the festival expect certain behaviour, decorum, and dress from the competitors? Also, have you given some consideration to the ages and backgrounds of the adjudicators?"

The other adults sat smiling and waited for the girls to answer. The girls looked at each other.

"But that's not fair! This is the year 2000 and we should be able to wear what we want!" exclaimed Caitlin.

Trent nodded his head. "I don't know if it's fair or not girls, but I have discovered in business that whether we like it or not, people expect us to put forward a certain image. Don't you want to do well? Maybe even win? I'm sure that you are very good dancers."

"Yes, we are! Our dance instructor says that someday we can turn professional," said the girls in unison.

Trent looked across the table into Thea's eyes as he spoke, "Well, think about it. Look at how your mother dresses and listen to her."

Caitlin held up the pretty shimmering outfit in front of her, shrugged her shoulders, and then slowly put it back in the bag. Her sister followed suit.

"Thank you, Mr. Krause. Mom, Grandma, we're sorry. I guess we were way off base. We'll take them back tomorrow, but I still think they're kind of cute," Caitlin said.

Joyce whispered in Thea's ear.

Thea grinned as she rose out of her seat and walked around behind the girls. She leaned over to hug and kiss both of them. Then she looked up at Trent and whispered, "Thank you."

Trent whispered back, "You're welcome. Thank you for letting me help."

Thea lifted one of the outfits out of the bag and examined it. "They're kind of cute, girls, just not appropriate for the festival. Maybe you could wear them privately when you practise your dance numbers in our basement or in Grandpa George's garage."

The twins energetically leaped from their seats and gave their mom a big kiss and a hug.

"Thanks, Mom!" they exclaimed in unison.

Joyce looked at the girls and said, "Your mom is busy. Let's go get a bite and then I'll take you shopping. I understand there are some new stores in the airport. Would you like to check them out?"

"Yes!"

"Thea, your dad and Brock are going to check on your airplane," Joyce continued.

Brock and George looked at each other in astonishment and said in unison, "We are?"

Joyce glared at them and cast her eyes at Thea and Trent. The two men quickly rose out of their seats. Brock extended his hand to Trent who stood up.

"Well, Trent, it's been a pleasure meeting another self-made businessman."

George added, "I enjoyed our chat. Take care!"

Brock put his hand on Trent's arm and whispered, "She's special, Trent. Thea is like a daughter to me."

Brock then turned and left, walking briskly toward the escalator.

George whispered, "She's my only daughter and I'm a very protective father, Trent. I hope you and Thea have a good chat."

George then left and caught up with Brock at the escalator leaving Trent and Thea at the table with Joyce and the girls.

"Come on, girls, let's go shopping," said Joyce as she rose out of her chair.

Caylen crossed her arms, looked at Trent and Thea, and then said, "Grandma, I like Mr. Krause. I think I'll stay here."

"Caylen!"

"Just kidding! I'm coming! I'm coming!"

Trent and Thea sat silently watching Joyce with the girls in tow hustling down the escalator. Outside nightfall had come. Thea and Trent sat sipping their coffee as they stared off through the huge windows that overlooked the runways, watching the airplanes land and takeoff. The airport had become a kaleidoscope of colourful lights designating the runways, service vehicles and the men guiding the airplanes to the access gateways.

Finally, Trent glanced at Thea. "Your daughters are great kids, Thea, and obviously very talented. What does your husband work at?"

Thea's eyes filled with tears as she took a deep breath and folded her arms over her chest as if to hold herself together, then she began to talk. "Phil was killed in an airplane crash three years ago last March. He was delivering supplies to a missionary's clinic in the South Pacific on behalf of the company and an engine malfunctioned. The kids and I live in a condominium near my parents' house. Mom and dad help me take care of Caitlin and Caylen. In fact, ever since Phil died they've given the girls and me constant support."

Compassion showed in Trent's eyes as he listened intently to Thea. Inside he felt that a doorway had been opened and his heart began to sing. He felt an overwhelming sense of relief.

"Dear, rough-edged, compassionate Brock has been like a second father to me. I would never have taken this position in Calgary if it hadn't been for Brock's constant support and encouragement. I overheard what Brock and dad whispered to you. Please don't take them too seriously. It's just that, well, for some reason they think they have to protect me, but I can take of myself. Mind you it's nice that they care enough to look out for me.

Trent, I'm sorry for rattling on. I must be boring you."

Trent's lips spread into a boyish grin. "No, I'm enjoying hearing about your family. It's kind of nice finally to have a chance just to sit and listen to you talk. Mind you, I'm a little jealous of you."

Thea looked into Trent's eyes noticing how they radiated warmth, but at the same time a sense of loneliness.

"What do you mean? Don't you have a family that cares for you?"

Trent looked away from Thea and downward at his coffee mug. His voice had a touch of sadness as he spoke, "I'm afraid not, Thea. There never has been a wife or children. Fifteen years ago, my parents were killed on that miserable stretch of road the government calls a highway just east of Golden. I love kids and am always helping with the children's charities in Abbottsford, but I don't have any kids of my own. It's the same old sad story about an ambitious man who has achieved all his dreams only to discover that his priorities were slightly out-of-whack, and now he discovers that his married friends are happier than he is with their families and three-bedroom bungalows. I envy you, Thea—your life is so full with your girls, your parents, and your job."

Thea and Trent lapsed into silence as they stared out of the big windows seeing, but not seeing, the huge jets thunder down the runway.

For some inexplicable reason Thea thought about the wise advice that dear Brock had tried to make her contemplate. *'Don't make the mistake I did and immerse yourself in work to the exclusion of all else. It's time to get on with your life, Thea.'*

She thought about her sweet precious daughters and how they needed her to guide them through the trials and tribulations of growing up. But then she glanced at Trent and memories of Phil flowed through her mind. She felt a deep longing again to experience the unbridled passionate love that Phil had freely given her for twelve joyful years. She had been the centre of his universe. Loving and cherishing Thea, he had made her the queen of his heart. She would often catch him staring at her and ask him why he was looking at her. He would just smile and say, *'Just wanted to make sure that you're still here. Sometimes when pilots come back, the people they love have left, gone on to other things or died.'* Thea thought to herself that she always responded to Phil in the same way. *'I will always be here for you, my beloved. I'm part of your life and you're part of mine forever and forever.'* Thea smiled as she remembered that she and Phil had had that little conversation daily.

It was their little ritual to remind them of their love for each other and it always started with Phil looking lovingly at Thea. She glanced again at Trent and found him looking at her in the same way that Phil always had. The colour rose in her cheeks and she cast her eyes down at the table where she rested her hands. She was surprised when Trent's large masculine hands covered hers.

Overwhelmed with emotion, Thea's voice quavered, "I can't." Then slowly, reluctantly, she eased her hands away from his and brushed away a tear. She leaned her head against the palms of her hands. "I'm sorry, I can't. There's just no space left in my life for anything, but my family and my job. I'm sorry Trent."

"Thea, can't we just be friends?"

Thea raised her head, wiped her eyes with a tissue, and then looked at Trent. He searched her eyes for some sign of willingness, some opportunity for them to come together.

"Thea, I would love to see you again even if it's just for coffee. It's not that far to fly from Abbottsford to Calgary."

Thea stared at Trent for a few lingering moments, then turned her head. "Trent, I've only looked at one other man and felt the way I did when I saw you in Concourse A and I married the guy. But that was eons ago. Now, I have two growing impressionable daughters to raise and a job. It just wouldn't be fair to you to allow our relationship to develop."

Trent leaned forward in his seat and captured Thea's slim hands in his. He spoke slowly. "Thea, I don't begin to understand why I feel the way I do about you, but I do know that if I lose you then something beautiful will have passed out of my life. This has never happened to me before. All I know is that I want to see you again."

Thea's lips quivered and her eyes again filled with tears, but she didn't say a word as she continued to study the huge jets through the large windows.

An announcement reverberated throughout the terminal. "All passengers for Dominion Air Flight 649 to Regina please report to Concourse A. The flight will leave in thirty minutes."

Trent sat solemnly looking at Thea. "May I come to Calgary to see you, Thea?"

"No, it's okay, Trent. Don't make a special trip. Sometime when you are in Calgary we'll probably bump into each other around the terminal. After all, this is where I work."

Saying nothing more Trent got up, picked up his briefcase and travel bag, and then stood looking longingly down at Thea for a few moments. Suddenly, he put his luggage back down and impulsively leaned forward to smooth back her golden hair, then he gently kissed her on the forehead.

Trent wrapped his arms around her. Hugging her, he whispered, "Goodbye."

Abruptly he turned and walked away toward the escalator that would start him on his journey to the airplane. Tears sprung from Thea's eyes and freely coursed down her cheeks as she sat staring mournfully at Trent's retreating figure.

A group of Dominion Air technicians sat in the Food Fair watching every detail of the exchange that had taken place between Thea and Trent.

Rick hunched his massive shoulders, leaned forward menacingly toward his men, then growled in his deep bass voice, "I think our Stock Officer deserves her privacy—what do you think guys?"

Several voices quickly exclaimed, "Yes, sir, I definitely agree! Let's give the lady some privacy."

Rick glared at his crew as he slowly raised his two-hundred-and-fifty-pound body of rock hard muscle from his seat. Dominion Air's technicians took the hint and quickly started down the escalator toward Concourse A.

Turning to look at Thea from the top of the escalator, Rick thought to himself, *'We are all like family in Dominion Air and I don't like it when somebody upsets one of us. When Brock promoted Thea over me to be the Stock Officer, I thought he was nuts. We've had many a disagreement, she and I, but in the end she won my respect. Now, I think that so-called gentleman and I will be having a little talk.'*

* * *

Joyce and the girls who had just returned from shopping lingered at a far corner of the Food Fair. They watched as Thea gradually leaned her head back into the palms of her hands.

Caylen looked inquisitively at her grandma while Caitlin whispered, "Grandma, what's wrong with mom?"

Wiping her eyes, Thea looked longingly toward the doors leading into Concourse A. Suddenly Caitlin left the others and marched over to Thea followed by Joyce and Caylen.

"Caitlin, get back here. Let's give your

mother a few minutes alone."

Caitlin's mouth was firmly set in a frown as she leaned over to kiss her mother on her cheek. Thea's eyes registered surprise as she turned to look up at her mom and her daughters.

Caitlin's voice took on a stern parental tone as she spoke to Thea, "Mom, why are you crying?"

"It's okay, Caitlin. I'm just upset. Maybe I'm just tired."

"I saw the way Mr. Krause looked at you. Where did he go? Caylen and I really liked him. Grandma thinks you should set your cap for him—whatever the heck that means."

Thea dried her tears; reached upward to run her fingers along the sides of her daughters' cheeks, then kissed them. "Thank you, Caitlin, Caylen, Mom, for your support, but ladies you are incurable romantics and not very practical. Trent has a huge company to manage and charities that he supports. I'm a widow with two daughters and a demanding job. I have no time, no room for romantic escapades."

Joyce and the girls sat down opposite Thea. Placing her hands over Thea's, Joyce looked deeply into her daughter's sombre eyes. Her voice took on a nostalgic tone as she started to talk, "Fifteen years ago, you met a wonderful man named Phil. You were in your first year of University Studies. George and I were so proud of you…a beautiful young lady and a Bachelor of Administration student. Then you introduced us to Phil. We, of course, worried about you, but thought you wouldn't let your relationship with Phil interfere with your studies. You shocked us by announcing that you and Phil were going to get married. At first we were numbed by the news, but that changed once we got busy with the wedding plans. It was so joyful to share your happiness when the big day came and you were such a beautiful bride. I haven't seen another man look at you the way Phil did until I watched Trent stare at you today. You and Phil pitched in to help Brock and your dad get Dominion Air off the ground—no pun intended. Remember the fun we had filling in at different positions for the guys? You amazed all of us by continuing your studies at night classes and completing your MBA with honours, plus you managed to find the time to raise two wonderful daughters. Phil used to constantly extol your virtues as a great wife. So what, Thea, do you mean you haven't time for romance?"

Thea sat watching young couples stroll hand and hand past the food kiosks enjoying each other's company as they made their food choices.

She turned to gaze deeply into her mother's eyes. "Mom, I don't know why I feel the way I do, but you know there *is* something special about Trent."

"Honey, if you feel something special about Trent, then go to him. You're right—I'm an incurable romantic, but you know your dad and I have always found that over the last forty years that no matter how tough things get, our love is the glue that always holds us together. It's that love that permits us to deal with any challenge that life throws our way, but honey, life gives us very few opportunities to experience that special love. When it comes along, you'd better grab on to it and hold on."

Caitlin crossed her arms over her chest. "Yeah, Mom, instead of sitting like a bump on a log—get going and find him!" she said.

Caylen leaned back mimicking her sister. "Ditto! Besides, he's neat! Grandma and grandpa are always there for us, but it would be nice to have a man's opinion once in a while."

Despite the gravity of the situation, Thea's lips curled upward in a tiny smile. "Your grandfather is a man who would do anything to help you with your problems."

"Yeah, but Mr. Krause is closer to our age and grandpa is a bit out of touch on some things. I mean, I love grandpa, but...well, you know what I mean."

Thea looked at Joyce as they shook their heads and smiled.

"Girls, I don't think it would be the best move to tell your grandfather that he's out of touch!" warned Thea. "Okay?"

The girls looked at each other and then nudged each other. "Okay!" they said in unison.

Thea slowly got to her feet. She happened to glance out of the huge windows. A Boeing 727 emblazoned with the Dominion Air insignia was just being backed away from its gate. A sudden gasp escaped her lips. Joyce immediately glanced out of the window, her eyes following Thea's. Then, she placed an arm around Thea's shoulders.

"It's Trent, isn't it, Thea?"

"Yes, Mom," Thea replied. Her face displayed a deep sense of sadness and regret as her eyes followed every movement of the airplane.

"It's all right, honey." Joyce touched her chest with her free hand. "In my heart I know that he'll come back."

Thea sat back down and adjusted her hair. Then she smoothed down her sweater.

Shaking her head she replied, "No, Mom. We will never see Trent again. You were right, I should have taken the chance when it came along."

Thea, Joyce, Caitlin, and Caylen sat watching as the Boeing carrying Trent accelerated down the runway until it broke free of gravity's power and soared gracefully into the air. The airplane made an eastern turn toward Saskatchewan then quickly it became a tiny speck just before it broached the horizon and was lost from sight. Joyce looked down at her watch then at her twin granddaughters.

"Thea, it's getting late and these wonderful grandchildren have school tomorrow."

Thea leaned over and embraced her daughters.

"Grandma's right, girls, it's time you headed home. I should be along in about an hour. Come on, Mom, let's rescue dad from Brock. Brock is probably filling his ear with a bunch of first-rate reasons as to why he should rejoin the company."

As the women walked down toward the

doors that opened into Concourse A, Thea's radio crackled.

"Ms. Tipton, this is Rick. Another one of our Boeing 727 airplanes has developed some strange instrument malfunctions. Would you come down and join me at Gate A16?"

Thea removed the radio from her belt. "I'm on my way, Rick! Sorry, ladies, but duty calls. I'll see you later at home."

Just as Thea started to walk into Concourse A, Brock and George sporting large grins came walking through the exit.

"Sorry, girls, that we took so long," said George. "We had to calm Rick down before we left."

George immediately stopped talking when he saw the look on Brock's face.

"What was Rick's problem, Dad?" Thea asked as she studied the expressions on the two men's faces.

"Oh, it was nothing, honey. It was just one of those situations where a passenger appeared to have been extremely nasty to a female employee. Rick decided that the passenger needed to be corrected, but it turned out to be just a misunderstanding. Brock and I smoothed everything over. Don't you worry about it."

"Well, Rick can be pretty darn intimidating. I hope it's okay."

Brock patted Thea on the shoulder as he said, "It is, Thea. Don't worry about it."

The radio crackled again and Rick's voice

blared forth, "Ms. Tipton, are you on your way?"

"Yes, Rick. I'm just entering Concourse A."

George grinned at Joyce. "Joyce, I've convinced Brock to stay the night with us."

Brock held up his hand with his fingers making the peace sign and quickly stated, "Joyce, his idea not mine."

Joyce laughed as she grinned at the men. "Of course you're welcome, Brock. George has some of his homemade Chardonnay wine that we can all share after the girls hit the sack and Thea gets home."

Caitlin stood with arms akimbo as she strongly stated, "Caylen and I are thirteen-years-old. We should get wine as well!"

Joyce shook her head, "Not this time, girls. You can have a sip on special occasions, but not tonight. You're too young to be having wine on a regular basis. Anyway, let's get going and let your mom get her job done. Thea, the girls can sleep over tonight. See you at our house."

"Goodbye everybody!" Thea said. Then she turned to walk through security and into Concourse A.

"Goodbye, Mom," cried the twins.

After Thea had disappeared into the inner recesses of Concourse A, Joyce whirled around to face the two men. "All right, guys, let's hear it."

"Hear what?" George responded in an innocent sounding voice.

"The truth as to why Rick was so upset.

Which passenger was he upset with? Oh no! Let me guess. It was Trent, wasn't it?"

Brock grinned and put his hand gently on Joyce's arm.

"Joyce, it seems that Rick saw Trent and Thea talking. Apparently when Trent left, Thea dissolved into tears and, well, Rick didn't like seeing a gentleman leave his lady boss in tears."

"Brock, what in heavens name did Rick do?"

"Well, he went searching for Trent in the concourse. He thought that Trent was probably gone because Flight 649 had just pulled out, but he found Trent sitting in a corner all by himself. Apparently he confronted Trent. He told him to get his posterior off the seat and come with him, but Trent refused. Rick demanded that Trent apologize to Thea, but Trent told him to mind his own business because he hadn't done anything to her. Well, when George and I saw the two of them nose to nose arguing, we decided to intercede."

Joyce scrutinized George and Brock noticing for the first time how George held a hand to his side and Brock covered his chin with a hand.

"All right, Brock, then what happened."

"Joyce, you would have been so proud. Rick had his arm held up in the air like he was going to punch out Trent's lights and George was just like a superhero. He dashed gallantly into the fray. Leaping up in the air, he grabbed Rick's arm. Rick is such a powerhouse. He swung his arm to get George off and George kind of took a little trip through the air. Your husband landed on some seats a few feet away from Rick. I think my buddy may have bruised a few ribs. Later, Rick explained to us that he always waves his arms around when he gets upset, but that he certainly was not going to punch Trent. Rick feels really bad about what happened."

"George, honey, are you all right? Honestly, why a man of your age would get between two athletic men like Trent and Rick is beyond me. Brock, what on earth is wrong with your jaw?" asked Joyce.

Brock looked at the floor with an embarrassed look on his face. "I got in front of Trent to keep him from attempting to punch out Rick. I guess I startled Trent and the next thing I remember was Trent helping me up and telling me how sorry he was that he had knocked me out cold right on the floor of the concourse. The most embarrassing part was explaining to the City Police Airport Unit that it was all a misunderstanding and that everything was fine."

Joyce started to laugh then said, "Next time you two decide to be heroes perhaps you should use your mouths. Guys, where is Trent?"

Brock and George looked at each other with smiles on their faces.

"Honey, he's sort of in Concourse A."

"Sort of, what do you mean, sort of?" asked Joyce.

"Brock, Rick, and I talked to Trent for a good half-hour. I don't understand it, but the guy just met Thea and he's crazy for her. Rick came up with a great idea to get them back together. Anyway, Joyce, can we get going? My ribs are starting to kill me."

"George, I want to know what you clowns have set up for Thea and Trent."

Joyce turned to talk to Brock and found that he had disappeared. "Now where in heavens name has Brock gone to?"

"Brock has gone to help Rick with our plan. Come on, let's go. I'll tell you all about it on our way home."

"Grandma, we want to wait up for mom and hear all the details about their date," gushed Caylen.

"Caylen, it's just a chance for the two of them to talk for few minutes."

Caitlin giggled as she flung her arms around her grandma's shoulders. "Maybe they will hug and I'll bet mom will let Mr. Krause give her a kiss."

Joyce rolled her eyes toward the ceiling and shook her head. "Let's go, girls."

Then they all turned and headed for the Plus-15 that would give them access to the Parkade.

* * *

As Thea walked rapidly through the large, cavernous, almost-empty concourse, she felt completely alone. A deep sorrow swirled around the centre of her inner core and threatened to burst free.

Approaching Rick's large figure at Gate

A16 she thought, *'All right, Ms. Tipton, let's suck it up! You've cried enough tears. Get control of yourself and whatever situation you have down here.'*

She straightened her back, squared her shoulders, smoothed back her errant lock of hair that always seem to fall out of place, and marched up to Rick with a look of firm determination.

"Hi, Rick. What's happening?" inquired Thea.

"Ms. Tipton, my crew and I found the problem in the instrument panel and replaced a faulty module. Strangely enough it was the very same part as the one on the 727 we just repaired and sent on its way to Regina. Anyway, I'm just going on board to conduct some final checks and wanted you to come along. I have a new technologist I want you to meet."

Thea felt waves of exhaustion spreading throughout her body and she shook her head. "Rick, it's getting late. I'm sure I can meet your man just as well tomorrow. Besides, it sounds to me like you have everything under control."

Rick scratched his full beard then ran his fingers through his unruly hair.

"Well, you see, Ms. Tipton, it's just that the new technologist heard some of the other guys talking about you being a great Stock Officer. They told him that of all the airlines, we have the best looker for a boss around."

Thea's face turned crimson red and her voice became as cold as ice. "Rick, I will not be paraded around like some beauty contestant."

At that, she whirled around to stride away, but Rick moving quickly for a man of his stature blocked her by circling around in front of her. He held up a massive hairy hand in a stop position.

"Ms. Tipton, with all due respect, you are dead wrong. Yes, when I first heard that Brock had chosen you over me to be the new Stock Officer, it was one big shock and I guess I was very resentful. I've known you and your family ever since you were a cute little girl with your blonde hair down to your waist, traipsing around after George. I just couldn't imagine you fulfilling the requirements of a Stock Officer. I thought Brock must be out of his ever-loving mind to choose a woman that could grace the pages of any of those glamour magazines. I mean, a Stock Officer makes our operations tick and must command respect from all our personnel. You just don't look like a Stock Officer. Well, man, I don't think I'll ever forget the first time one of my guys screwed up. You hauled his and my butt up on the carpet really quickly. Mine because I was his boss. Ever since then the guys have grown to respect your brains and toughness. You are our leader, but I'll bet no other airline has a Stock Officer with your looks. The men love to show you off as a woman who— excuse the expression—is one great looker, but also a woman who is one great boss who cares for all of us. I remember when John, my son, was sick. You did everything possible to make sure that my wife and family were fine. Ms. Tipton, you've proven yourself over and over. So what do you think? Would you come and talk to the new guy for a few minutes?"

Thea stood looking at Rick then despite being emotionally drained and very tired, she forced a small smile and quietly said, "Rick, thank you for the compliments. I'm sorry if I overreacted. It's just that I try so hard to do an excellent job and I guess after a day like today my emotions are worn a bit thin." Thea touched one of Rick's massive arms and tilted her head back to look up at him. "Rick, I wish you would relax and call me Thea. Team partners should be on a first-name basis. Yes, I would like to meet our new man and then I am heading home."

The two of them entered the airplane. Seeing the man in dirty coveralls working in the cockpit with his back to them, Thea called out, "Hello! My name is Thea Tipton, Stock Officer of Dominion Air."

The man never turned around, but quietly responded by saying, "Hello Ms. Tipton. It's an honour to make your acquaintance. Excuse me for just a minute. I'm almost done here."

Thea walked over to one of the airplane's first class seats and sat down. "I'll just sit here and wait for you as long as you won't be too long."

"I'll be right out, Ms. Tipton." The man reached up as if to adjust something near the window of the cockpit.

Suddenly, Thea's radio crackled and Brock's booming voice filled the stillness in the aircraft, "Thea, where are you?"

"Rick and I are in the Boeing 727 checking out a problem."

"Thea, would you send Rick out to the fifteen-minute parking at Departures? I'm sorry, but I forgot to give you some reports from personnel."

"Okay, Brock."

Rick shook his tousled head. "I'll be right back."

He walked out of the airplane leaving Thea alone in the airplane with the technician, who appeared to be done his task as he gathered up some tools and generally tidied up the cockpit. Outside the door of the airplane Rick joined Brock, smiled, and together they walked up the ramp leading into the concourse. Inside Thea watched as the new man turned to walk toward her. Her mouth dropped open in surprise, then she smiled as she subconsciously raised a hand to smooth back her blonde hair from her eyes.

"Trent, what on earth are you doing here?"

Trent sat down in a seat across the aisle from Thea. "I seem to have gotten on the wrong airplane."

Thea's deep blue eyes stared at him as she shook her head. "That's silly, Trent. How on earth could anyone as clever as you do such a thing?"

Trent glanced down at his hands then back at Thea. "I guess that excuse does sound a bit unbelievable. How about the excuse that Brock has given me a job as a technician and now I work for you?"

"You're not qualified, Trent. I'm afraid that you wouldn't last one hour"

"The truth is, Thea, I couldn't leave without finding someway of seeing you again. I love being with you. There's something very special between us, Thea. Listening to you talk about your job and your family made me feel good. Helping the girls with their problem made me feel that I was part of your family, if only for just a few minutes. I know I could never be a dad to Caylen and Caitlin, but it felt good to be needed. I guess that sounds pretty corny, but it's the truth."

Thea smiled at Trent then turned her head to gaze down the aisle toward the cockpit.

"There's nothing wrong with this airplane…is there, Trent?" She sat waiting patiently for him to answer.

He glanced at her through the corners of his eyes and then stared back down at his hands. "No, I imagine that you know it's the airplane that Brock flew in on today."

Thea nodded her head. "Yes, I knew that. After all, I am the Stock Officer. It's my business to know everything about our equipment and operations."

"So, why did you go along with Rick?"

Placing her hand on top of her heart, Thea replied, "I guess something in here told me that it was important for me to board this airplane. It looks like my intuition was correct, but the question is, what happens next?"

"You're not mad at the guys and me for

setting this up?"

"No, as impractical as this rendezvous is, everyone meant well."

Slowly Trent spoke. "Thea, I desperately want you to be part of my life. If you feel the same way, I'm sure that our futures will be together—no matter what the obstacles. Thea...will you have supper with me?"

Thea's eyes filled with tears. "Trent, fifteen years ago I asked a man named Phil whom I had met by chance to go out with me, and thank God, he said 'yes.' Back then I was so happy that I cried. I never thought I'd feel this way about anyone again. Now you and I have met by chance."

Trent's hand reached across the aisle to firmly grasp Thea's. He lovingly kissed the back of her hand.

Thea thought about how a chance meeting with a man in dirty, scruffy overalls had swept her off her feet fifteen years ago.

Then she smiled as she looked up into Trent's eyes and whispered, "Yes."

THE BLACK TUNNEL

I had desperately cried out for help to Bret Richards,
The man who wore the shield,
But he wouldn't listen to my concerns about Edgar Bradley,
Said he couldn't help without corroborating evidence,
Just a girl's fanciful story.

Then Bradley snared me in his Black Tunnel,
The terror of the Black Tunnel clouded my mind,
I couldn't take Constable Richards there,
Said he couldn't help without corroborating evidence,
Just a girl's fanciful story.

Cruelly he dismissed me. Cast me aside.
He had no trust in me.
My family trusted in my word,
They healed my body and soul,
My family brought me back with kindness and understanding.

Then my family dealt with Bradley, the monster.
My family took in my child,
Cared for us, and gave us life,

My family helped me move on
Past the terror and degradation.

Twelve years have passed, and now the same monster threatens Tara.
I will not cry out for help to Bret Richards,
The man who wears the tarnished shield,
I say, "Destroy Bradley, the monster,
So that my sweet and beautiful child may live!"

* * *

In September 1987, Constable Chris McNeil of the Calgary Police Service met with Chief Constable Al Breckenridge. After the meeting, Chris's pencil-thin moustache curled upward as he squared his massive shoulders and smiled broadly. He rode the elevator down to the sixth floor and walked briskly down the hall back to his small cubicle. He had just settled down to work on a staggering pile of reports at his desk when his partner, Bret Richards, poked his closely-shaven head around the corner. Bret's eyes seemed to dance with anticipation. He displayed a broad grin as he greeted his long-time friend and partner.

"Hey, Buddy, I see you're finally done hobnobbing with the brass on the tenth floor. I assume they told you that we're being transferred to District Two?"

"We're being split up, Bret. I've been assigned to Willow Valley Elementary Junior High in District Two as the Youth Liaison Officer."

"You've got to be kidding! You're going to be a *kiddy cop*? I'll bet Chief Breckenridge's devious mind made that happen. What the blazes does Al think he's doing by pulling experienced cops off the streets? We're short-handed as it is. I was counting on us working together on some of our long-standing cases. Well, I suppose that twenty years on the street must entitle you to this vacation with pay, eh?"

Chris stared at the ceiling, shook his head and then leaned forward glaring at Bret.

"Bret, you're dead wrong. Working with kids is *real* police work. Kids need to see the uniform at times other than just when they're in trouble."

"Chris, wake up and smell the roses! We wear the shield to enforce the law, not to act as glorified social workers, babysitters, or teachers. Well, anyway, I guess if that's what you want. Good luck, Buddy! As for me, I'm going to that new facility in District Two—just a few blocks from your school—to do some *real* police work as the Staff Sergeant."

"Buddy, do you know that that *new* facility is really a renovated old mansion up on the west side of Willow Valley? Apparently the Mantino family donated the land, the building and the cost of the renovations to the City of Calgary for the Police Service. The whole project didn't cost our City Fathers one red cent!"

Chris clasped Bret's right hand in his own

massive grip. He laughed at his long-time buddy, "Well, anyway, I guess if that's what you want. Good luck, Buddy!"

"You know, Chris, I can't figure out why the Mantinos would want to assist the Police Service, but I guess wonders will never cease. Anyway, don't be a stranger at the district office. I expect to see your ugly mug every couple of days in my office for coffee, and that's an order!"

A week later, the two friends reported to their new assignments.

* * *

On a blustery morning in November, a frigid wind was howling down Willow River Valley when, about noon, Chief Al Breckenridge arrived in his command car to pick up the Assistant Principal, Kevin McManus, at Willow Valley Elementary Junior High.

In the slightly-built balding Kevin, he had found a strong supporter. When Chief Breckenridge had posted Chris McNeil to Willow Valley School, Kevin had repeatedly encouraged Chris in his efforts to work with the students. Chris was known as a *gentle giant* by his fellow constables. In the school patrol, he was very active in promoting leadership and citizenship training. The kids affectionately and respectfully referred to him, behind his back of course, as *Big Chief*.

As Kevin and Chief Breckenridge rode in the sleek command car to the new police district office where the school's monthly patrol award ceremony would be conducted, Chief Breckenridge turned toward Kevin. "Kevin, I want to thank you for your support—specifically of Chris, and generally of my youth liaison officers. However, I'm afraid that a severe cutback is imminent. I have to justify the assignment of manpower to work with young people. Unfortunately, my senior district officers—both the District Two Inspector and the Staff Sergeant—tend to make their recommendations based on statistical patterns and totals of the different types of reactive calls taken by the troops. Also, I'm dealing with an attitudinal problem. The feeling is prevalent in the ranks that assignments to the Youth Liaison Unit are rewards for effective police work. In other words, if you are good on the streets then as a reward it's a nice break if you can become a kiddy cop for the short term."

"Excuse me, Al, but isn't that a bunch of unmitigated nonsense? I agree that totally professional police officers must react effectively to calls, but also they must make it their business to deal effectively with people on a day-to-day basis. Kids need to see officers out in the community and feel confident in approaching them."

"I agree, Kevin, but then again, it's an officer like Staff Sergeant Richards who needs to be convinced, not me. I would ask a favour of you. It would be very much appreciated if you would write down and pass along some anecdotes of Chris's successes with the kids. Perhaps we can come up with something that will make believers out of our critics."

The two men arrived at the district office.

Bret Richards was seated near a window in the conference room. He was there along with the inspector, eighteen officers, the school patrollers, Susan Mantino—the grade six teacher and some parents. Suddenly, he spotted the lean lanky figure of the Chief unfolding himself to get out of the command car.

He muttered to himself, "Great Scott! Why didn't somebody tell us that Al was coming to this shindig?"

Leaping to his feet, his deep husky voice rang out, "Ladies and gentlemen of District Two! On your feet— the Chief is here!"

Pandemonium reigned supreme as the officers scrambled from their chairs and rushed around to find their hats and adjust their uniforms. In a matter of thirty seconds, the twenty officers stood rigidly at attention as the Chief, followed by Kevin, entered the room. At a signal from Chris, the parents and children stood to join the officers as a sign of respect for Chief Breckenridge.

Al stopped and gazed around at the group with a wide grin.

"Thank you, ladies and gentlemen, for that fine welcome, but we are gathered here to honour these very special children, not me. Please let's all mingle with the kids. I'm looking forward to eating pizza and visiting with our young friends."

He noted with pleasure that all of his ranking officers were present from District Two and the

Youth Liaison Unit. He was pleasantly surprised to observe that Susan Mantino's parents, Tony and Louisa Mantino, were sitting across from her. Tony's facial expression betrayed little emotion, but his penetrating deep-set eyes radiated power and seemed to be constantly assessing all in the room. He only permitted himself a smile when he fondly looked at his wife, or Susan and the beautiful young girl next to her. Louisa, by contrast, never stopped smiling as she spoke in Italian to Susan and the young girl and energetically gestured to make a point. Her face was dominated by wrinkles that extended upward from her eyes and mouth and gave the impression that she was constantly happy, far different from the rather dour appearance of her husband. Susan Mantino and the girl could have been twins except for their difference in ages. Both had long dark hair, slim figures, olive-coloured skin and dark expressive eyes. Chief Breckenridge went over and sat down next to the shy girl who immediately stared at her pizza. Chris quickly hustled over to the table and smiled broadly.

"Tara, it is my pleasure to introduce you to Chief Constable Breckenridge. Chief Breckenridge, this pretty young lady is Tara Mantino, Susan's daughter, and Tony and Louisa's granddaughter."

Tara continued to stare shyly at her food as she quietly whispered, "Hi."

Al leaned over and spoke in a quiet voice, "Mr. Mantino, thank you for your generosity in donating this fine building to the Calgary Police Service."

"Chief Breckenridge, please call me Tony. As for this property, it was just something that we didn't need. It is of no importance."

"Tony, it was a very important gesture on your part. Will you please call me Al?"

"Perhaps, but then again if an attempt at reconciliation is one-sided, it is of no consequence is it?"

"Tony, I have brought Constable McNeil to the school to help rebuild the bonds of trust between our people and your family."

"Yes, Constable McNeil is, as my granddaughter says, a neat guy. He listens well and seeks to understand us. I am surprised to learn that Sergeant Richards is Constable McNeil's friend. Sergeant Richards seems to be very dedicated to enforcing the law, but he has made no time available for sitting with our people. I'm surprised that he is back in our community after what happened to our Susie."

Susan glanced out of the corners of her eyes toward Bret Richards who was sitting quietly eating pizza with Kevin and a couple of school patrollers. She frowned, and then focussed her attention on her mother, Louisa, who with a great flurry of hand gestures was starting another story.

Al gazed thoughtfully out of the window then spoke, "Mr. Mantino—Tony— Bret Richards was made Staff Sergeant because he is an excellent investigative officer and administrator. He and Chris McNeil are close friends. Bret, I am sure, realizes the demands of this district and will come to use and appreciate Chris's skills in working with the community."

With a look of concern in her eyes, Tara turned to her mother.

"Mom, what did Sergeant Richards do to you?"

"He didn't do anything to me. Tara, please, just eat your pizza."

"What did grandfather mean by what happened to our Susie?"

"Tara!"

Tony Mantino leaned across the table and gently put his hand on Tara's. "Tara, this is painful for your mother. Later when you are older we will discuss this. Now, eat your pizza."

Susan stared into her father's eyes. Her eyes were moist and she quietly whispered, "Thank you, Papa."

Chief Breckenridge thought to himself that Chris must indeed have a special gift with people. He had managed to bring Louisa, Tony, Susan, and Bret together. True the Mantinos and Bret had not spoken to each other, but at least they were in the same room. It was a good start toward reconciliation. Perhaps the Mantinos' love for Susan and Tara overrode all else. They wanted to see their granddaughter receive her patrol award and for that they were willing to be in the same room as the officer toward whom they had harboured great bitterness for the past twelve years.

Chief Breckenridge continued quietly chatting with the Mantinos. Soon Chris called for silence and started the award ceremonies. He requested Staff Sergeant Richards to come forth and assist him in conducting the presentations. Initially Bret Richards sat rigidly in his chair and stared at his buddy. As he slowly and reluctantly rose from his chair, he smiled and mouthed the words, "I'll get you for this, Chris."

"Get up here, you big lug. You'll enjoy yourself."

By the end of the program Staff Sergeant Richards's face seemed to be frozen in a big smile as he enthusiastically assisted Chris in the presentations. Chris then announced that the Chief would assist Staff Sergeant Richards in presenting the *Patrolman of the Month* award to Tara Mantino. The patrollers, who had a deep affection for the quiet unassuming Tara, went wild pounding the tables and yelling out, "Way to go, Tara!"

Chris had asked a mother to take pictures of the gathering and the award ceremonies. He thought for a moment, moved over to the Mantino's table and then, choosing his words carefully, said, "Mr. Mantino, it would mean a great deal to Tara if you and your wife would join the Chief and Sergeant Richards for a picture. Susan, because you are Tara's teacher as well as her mother, I think it's appropriate for you to be included."

Susan's face turned white. She clenched her fists on her lap and vigorously shook her head.

Louisa smiled lovingly at Susan and then said in a soft voice, "Susie, look at our Tara standing up there so happy! Please let us not spoil her special moment."

"Mama, I don't know if I can smile around that man."

"Susie, baby, don't smile for him. Smile for your child."

Tony abruptly stood up and extended his hands to his wife and Susan. He grinned and said. "Come, let us show these people that the Mantinos are a handsome family."

The pictures were taken. The Mantinos and Sergeant Richards then quickly retired to their respective positions on the opposite sides of the room.

Later, Bret watched the parents leave the district office. Susan quietly lined up the children and led them back to the school.

Bret marched up to Chris and boisterously slapped him on the shoulder. "That was a great get-together, Chris! The kids were great. The pizza was great. Man, I don't think I can recall so many of us getting together except, of course, down at the Cuff and Billy Pub."

"It was terrific for the kids to see you and the guys here at the District. Thanks for having us, Bret."

"You're welcome, but don't think you've converted me. I still believe that the heart of being a great police officer is how you perform on the streets and how you react to various situations. Anyway, Buddy, you watch out for yourself! I have to get back on duty."

"See you, Bret. Watch your back!"

Later as Chief Breckenridge drove Kevin back to the school, he turned to him saying, "Tara is a lovely girl, Kevin. It was nice to see Tony and Louisa at the festivities."

"Yes, it was. Tony and Louisa have donated a great amount of time and money to the school. They are the main organizers of our multicultural food fairs and potlucks."

"It was a good move on Chris's part to have Bret Richards help to present the patrol awards. A lot of people wouldn't believe it, but Bret is really quite shy and awkward in social situations. In fact, it was great that Chris convinced Bret to host the patrol awards at the district office."

"Why's that?"

"Well, twelve years ago when I was Bret's District Two Inspector, we received a report from some of Susan Mantino's friends that she had been assaulted by Edgar Bradley and his teenage cohorts. Bradley's home is right across the street from the new district office. Bret was the senior investigative officer on the scene. However, when he tried to talk to Susan and her mother and father, they just didn't seem to relate to him or trust him. Susan muttered something about not wanting to deal with a police officer that wouldn't break bread with her family. She said her family would solve her problem. I don't know, maybe their attitude toward the police had something to do with them being new immigrants from Sicily. Bret checked what little information he could find out from Susan and her friends. We heard a rumour that Tony's family had dealt with Bradley, but Bradley never did lay any charges or ever say a word about any problems with the Mantinos. It's funny, but ever since that time Mr. Bradley has walked with a limp. Eventually the case was dropped for lack of corroborative evidence. I don't know. Given Bret's past problems with the Mantino family, maybe I should just transfer him for his own and everyone else's sake."

Chief Breckenridge stopped the sleek command car in front of the school. Kevin got out of the vehicle and leaned over to talk to him.

"Thanks, Al, for coming to today's festivities. It was very special for the kids to have you there. It's none of my business, but I have a suggestion. Bret Richards must be an excellent police officer to have achieved his present rank. Why don't you leave him in his present position and give him time to mend fences with the Mantino Family and their supporters? We have many cultural groups in the school and it's a tradition for our staff to invite the community and the agencies that assist us to join us for potlucks. Bret is going to find as he settles in as the new Staff Sergeant that his staff will expect him to go with them to our functions. After all, policemen love to eat and the food is great! And, as I have already said, Tony and Louisa Mantino are the main parent-organizers. Maybe the ice can be broken if Bret can interact with them on neutral turf at the school."

"Okay. I'll adopt a wait-and-see position in regard to Bret. See you, Kevin. Keep up the good work!"

* * *

A week after the patrol awards luncheon, Tara had a really rotten day. Susan, as usual, had driven her to school, but mysteriously Tara had missed her first two classes and she had received a late slip from Freida, the senior secretary. The Physical Education teacher noticed that Tara seemed to have some difficulty participating in the gym activities. The Social Studies teacher also reported that she saw Tara's boyfriend, Lorne, affectionately pat Tara on the back to say *hello* and heard her scream as if she were in severe pain. Then she swatted his hand away from her.

Early in the afternoon, Tara's class was in the music room with Susan when Tara began pouting. Suddenly, she absolutely refused to practise her dance solo for the upcoming Christmas Concert. Next, Susan had attempted to fit her for a dance costume, but Tara said she didn't like it and wouldn't try it on. When Susan encouraged her to cooperate, Tara marched out of the room and slammed the door.

Exasperated, Susan yelled, "Come back here, young lady!"

When Susan raced out into hallway she frantically looked right and left, but couldn't see Tara anywhere. She was just turning right to race down the staircase to the main floor when she was brought to an abrupt halt by Chris McNeil's massive bulk.

"Chris, I don't know what's the matter, but Tara has been having a really terrible day! First she gets a late slip from Freida for missing her first two classes, and then it seems as though all the teachers in the school have had troubles with her, including me."

"But why would she miss any of her classes?" Chris questioned. "I thought you drove her to school."

"I did!"

"Where was she during those first two hours of school?"

"I don't know, Chris, I haven't had a chance to sit her down and find out. Oh no! No, not again—not after all these years!"

"Susan, don't assume anything until we've had a chance to talk to her. Call Kevin and tell him you need someone to watch your class, then go to his office and wait there for me. I'll conduct a search of the school."

Chris had just finished searching the upper floor of the north end of the school and was standing inside the door of the library when he noticed somebody's long black hair through a gap between the books on one of the lower shelves.

He walked slowly over to the librarian and whispered, "Marlene, Tara is having some problems. Would you please take your students down to the computer lab? Then call Susan, she's in Kevin's office, and tell her I need some time alone with Tara."

After the other children had left with the librarian, Chris quietly walked over to Tara and stared down at her sympathetically. Tara's face was tear-stained and she had red blotches on her neck. She stared up at him with a look of fear and anger in her eyes. Slowly, he eased his six-foot-five inch frame onto the carpet beside her and stuck his long legs out in front of him.

He looked down at Tara, gave her a bunch of tissues and said, "Hi."

Fifteen minutes passed by and not another word was spoken. Finally, Chris began to speak, "Tara, let's go down to the staff room. Now I don't know about you, but when you're as big as I am, you get really hungry. Somebody told me that a group of parent volunteers in the office brought treats for the adults. Come on, we'll go prepare a tray of goodies and take them to Mr. McManus's office."

Tara sat and stared straight ahead. A single tear rolled down her cheek onto her pink cotton blouse.

"Come on, Tara, I need your help. I thought we were buddies."

Chris stood up and held out his hand to her. Tara turned to look up at Chris, her lower lip trembling as she nodded her head. She took his hand and stood up. When they arrived at the staff room, Tara had to smile in spite of herself as Chris made an elaborate display of preparing a tray of food. He busily extolled the virtues of the various squares and asked her which goodies her mother would like the best.

"This is indeed a special occasion for me to have you helping me. It's been a long time since I've had a chance to spend time with one of my favourite patrollers. We sure had a great time at the district office, eh? Did your grandparents and mom hang up your *Patrolman of the Month* certificate?"

Tara smiled and nodded her head.

"And I understand that you have a special dancing and singing part in the Christmas Concert. I was having coffee with Sergeant Richards and the other district officers yesterday. I was telling them about your talents and you know what, I think I've convinced them and their wives to come to the concert to see you."

Suddenly, Tara sat down on a staff room chair. Tears flowed from her eyes and words interspersed with sobbing sounds poured forth from her mouth. Chris kneeled and stared into her eyes.

Tara sobbed, "I was wandering along the edge of the field and three big high school girls grabbed me. They took me to the Black Tunnel and they hurt me. Please don't tell my mom or Mr. McManus. I don't want anyone to know, ever!"

"Tara, your mom will understand and Mr. McManus is always willing to listen to your problems."

"They won't believe me! They'll just think I'm making up a story."

"Tara, I believe you. Don't worry. I'll help you. Come on, let's give Mr. McManus and your mom a chance."

"All right, Big Chief. I'm sorry—I mean Constable McNeil."

As Chris and Tara entered Kevin's office, he was surprised to see Mr. and Mrs. Mantino. Susan's eyes had a deep look of concern in them as she spoke to Chris.

"Chris, I thought it best that my parents be present. I have a feeling that Tara's story may involve an old adversary. Tara, sweetheart, are you okay?"

"Mom, I'm sorry! I was so scared! I didn't mean to upset you. I'm sorry!"

Susan quickly knelt in front of Tara gathering her daughter into her arms.

"It's all right, sweetheart. Please, just tell us what's happened."

Susan then sat on one of the office chairs while Tara stood beside her and held her hand.

Chris sat down, stuck his feet out in front of him and looked around the room. He lowered his chin to his chest and then quietly spoke, "I would suggest that we all sit quietly and Tara, when you are ready, tell us your story. Okay?"

"All right."

As the group in the office waited, they could hear the cheery voices of the office secretaries and their parent volunteers faintly through the office door as they busily assembled the Christmas Concert Programs. On the other side of the office, they were aware of the low moaning sound of a warm Chinook wind and the branches of a Mayday tree rapping against the window in a stuttering, scratching manner.

After twenty minutes had passed, Tara dried her eyes with a tissue and began speaking in a soft halting voice, "Well, all right Big Chief—I mean Constable McNeil—I'll tell you—for all the good it will do."

"Big Chief is fine with me, Tara."

"This morning my mom drove me and dropped me off by the school grounds. As I was walking around the edge of the field, three big high school girls grabbed me. They said that I was lucky because Mr. Bradley wanted me to work for him. I know that working for Mr. Bradley means stealing things. Old Mr. Bradley takes a lot of the older high school girls to special things, but he has other reasons for taking them on those outings. The older girls make sure that the younger girls steal for Mr. Bradley. I told them *No Way*, but they said I'd get hurt *real bad* if I did anything stupid. Then those girls took me around the corner from the school and threw me into a long black car. They got in the car with me. A man dressed in a black suit was driving. He told me I had better lie down on the back seat or he would have to get rough with me. It seemed like we rode in the car for a long time. I was *so* scared!

When we got out of the car, I remember seeing a shovel on a wall, and smelling gas. The driver took me down a long flight of narrow stairs in the floor, then into the Black Tunnel that had faintly glowing lights. We walked a long way through the tunnel, past three doors on my right side, and then we came to a room with a green table in the centre.

Mr. Bradley was sitting in a chair by the green table. The wall behind the green table was covered with pictures of girls. Radios, TV sets and other things were stacked against one of the walls. He told the big girls to give me a taste of what I would get if I didn't steal for him. Two of the girls bared my back and bent me over the table and the third girl hit me on the back with something three times and then they told me to stand up.

Then Mr. Bradley got out of his chair and just stood there looking at me. Suddenly his face got a funny look on it and he screamed, "*You look just like her! You look just like Susan Mantino*!" He asked what my name was. When I told him, his face turned red, his eyes got all buggy and he looked really angry. He pushed each of the High School girls against the wall and kept yelling how stupid they were.

When his back was turned, I raced back into the tunnel. I saw a row of light switches and I turned them off. Everything went black. Mr. Bradley was yelling and swearing. I carefully moved along the wall until my hand felt a doorknob and I tried as hard as I could to open the door, but it was stuck. I planted my foot against the wall I pulled again and finally, it slowly opened. I went inside and quietly closed the door behind me. I had to brush away a lot of gross spider webs. As I moved forward, I tripped into some steps which led upward to a wooden door above my head. I pushed up until the door moved and then I could see daylight. I climbed out onto a platform that had a roof, but no walls. Then I raced back to the school as fast as I could. I was so scared and my back really hurt!"

Tara then sat on her mother's lap, buried her face into Susan's right shoulder and started to cry.

Susan's face had turned ashen as she stared out of the office window.

Tony's voice was a quiet whisper with a hard edge, "Chris, we will take Tara home right now. It would be best if she's not part of whatever happens next."

"Mr. Mantino, she can't leave yet. I need to get some investigative officers to come and hear her story."

Susan pulled Tara to her feet. She wrapped her arms around her and tenderly kissed her on the forehead.

"Chris, Tara is going home with her grand-parents until this problem is settled."

"Susan, she has to give a statement to the investigative officers."

"She can do that at our home."

"All right."

After Tara had left, Susan, Kevin, and Chris went to the staff room to discuss the situation. As the men sat talking, they noticed that Susan had wandered over to the window. Her hands shook as she placed them on the window frame and she stared out at the passing traffic. Finally, she dabbed her eyes with a tissue and quietly sat down opposite the two men.

Chris gazed solemnly at Kevin, "I have to phone the district office and ask for a car crew to come down to interview Tara. I know her story sounds extremely fanciful. I hope that she can identify the girls and take the officers to the tunnel. Without corroborating evidence, the guys will probably consider it to be a lot of smoke with no substance."

Kevin quietly shook his head. "Chris, the district constables will be lucky if they can get Tara to tell her story. She trusts us. She doesn't even know the district people."

"I know, Kevin, and another point is that Tara is accusing a powerful man of causing her to be physically assaulted. The Calgary Police Service applies the law equally to all, but before proceeding against Bradley the investigating officers will have to make darn sure that all their ducks are in a row."

"Listen, Chris! Tara's welfare is at stake. Do something. Help her!"

Susan stood and walked over to the staff room sink to wash her coffee cup. She turned toward the two men, her face red with anger. "Twelve years ago your friends in blue did nothing about Bradley. Tara and my parents will have reached home by now. My dad will be considering what actions to take against Bradley. After all, that's his granddaughter who was hurt by Bradley's gang. Chris...if you don't do something immediately, there will be war!"

Susan put her coffee cup into the cupboard,

slammed the door, wheeled around and charged out of the staff room.

Chris nodded and phoned the District Office. He spoke to his old pal Staff Sergeant Richards who indicated that he would go down to the Mantino's home with a female constable, Charlene Scappatura.

When the two investigating officers arrived at the Mantino's house, they attempted to talk to Tara in the presence of her grandparents in their front room. Thoughout the questioning Tara quietly stared at the floor. Finally, Bret and Charlene gave up and drove over to the school.

Later in Kevin's office, Bret looked at Kevin and Chris with a frown on his face as he shook his head. His deep voice rumbled as he growled, "Well, that was sure a waste of time. I don't know how you're supposed to help people if they won't even talk to you. My compadre and I are out of here."

"What about the bruises on Tara's back, Charlene?" inquired Chris.

"I could find no visible bruising on her back."

Bret commented, "I would say that if Tara *was* beaten, somebody knew how to hit without bruising, which means he or she has had a lot of experience in doing this stuff to girls. Don't get me wrong, guys, I've heard rumours about the charming Mr. Bradley, the master thief, and his despicable treatment of young girls, but without corroborating evidence there is nothing that can be done."

A few minutes later, Bret and Charlene left Kevin's office. They walked briskly down the hall and out of the parking lot door. As the two officers approached their squad car, they noticed Susan standing nearby, her slender silhouette framed in the sunshine. She was quietly watching them.

Charlene crossed her arms and leaned her elbows on the roof of the squad car. She stared into Susan's eyes. Susan's eyes expressed sorrow, loss and rage. Those eyes were hard and they deeply disturbed Charlene.

Charlene whispered, "Susan, did you have something that you wanted to tell the Staff Sergeant and me?"

"Yes. I'm twenty-six years old. When I was fourteen years of age Edgar Bradley was constantly bothering me. Finally, Bradley went too far and *I* became a victim of the Black Tunnel. Nobody came to my rescue and I was hurt—badly. Bradley uses one cane to walk with as a result of what he did. My family is Italian. You and the other policemen don't like us because you think we are all criminals. My folks worked hard for many years to build the largest general contracting construction company in Calgary. They live in their big house by the river because of their success, not because they are Mafia. We will take care of my daughter."

Bret walked quickly around the squad car. He stopped in front of Susan looming over her with a look of anger in his eyes. He sternly growled in his deep voice, "Miss Mantino, the Calgary Police Service does not have any prejudice against Italians.

I remember your case. The Service couldn't do anything because we had no corroborating evidence to support the story your friends told us about what happened. We talked to several people in the Italian community, but nobody would speak to us."

Susan stared up at Bret with a look of rage in her eyes.

"In my culture, friendships are made with people who take the time to sit and visit with us. Friendships are formed across a table with food and wine. The only time we ever saw you, Sergeant Richards, was after a crime was committed and then it was too late, wasn't it? We don't talk to those we don't trust. I repeat, my family will take care of my daughter. This time we will take care of the threat of Edgar Bradley permanently!"

Tears gathered around Susan's dark eyes and her face reddened. Her voice suddenly changed from that of a calm collected professional to one filled with a mixture of rage and sorrow. "He will not be allowed to harm my sweet Tara. He will be stopped! Do you hear? He's a monster! Now, I would suggest that you leave. Just go away! I have my last class to teach."

Bret and Charlene stood for several minutes staring at Susan as she wheeled around and raced back into the school. Then the officers silently slid into their car and drove off.

As Bret drove the powerful sleek blue-and-white toward the district office, Charlene glanced in his direction.

"Sergeant Richards, have you ever received

an invitation from the Mantino family for supper?"

"Yes, a few invitations. About twelve or thirteen years ago."

"Did you go?"

"No."

"Why not?"

"Darn it, Charlene, you know what our job is like! Day in and day out we are answering calls. If I start zapping around the district attending suppers, we lose our effectiveness. We just won't keep up. I don't know! Maybe I should have gone. One old Italian gentleman said to me that I had spat upon the friendship of the Mantino family by refusing to break bread with them. Tony, Louisa and their friends made me feel like an outsider in my own district!"

"Sergeant...things are going to get much worse if you don't repair the damage with the Mantinos."

"What do you mean *get worse*?"

"Did you know that ninety-eight per cent of the five thousand employees who work in the Mantino Construction Company are Italian? Of course, one must also consider the number of friends and supporters of the Mantinos. In their eyes, you failed the governing family, the Mantinos, twelve years ago and they probably hold you responsible for what happened to Susan. I'm Italian and believe me when Susan says that her family will take care of Edgar Bradley—it will happen. Edgar and his gang of lady thieves are in for some rough one-way rides. They are going to wish that they'd never laid a hand on Tara or Susan. Bret, you're my Sergeant and with all due respect I would suggest that you do something quickly."

Bret stared through the windshield with a frown on his face.

"Sometimes this job is the pits. I thought I was doing a great job, but I guess I didn't take the time to get to know and understand the very people whom I serve as a police officer."

"Bret, do you have Mr. Mantino's private telephone number?"

"Yes."

"I would suggest that you phone him when we get back to the district office."

"Why? He probably wouldn't talk to me anyway."

"Well, maybe you can get him to come to the district office. They live right next door."

"I guess it's worth a try."

* * *

Meanwhile, Susan had left the school and had gone to join her daughter and her parents. Chris, who was sitting with Kevin in his office, decided that he would phone the Mantinos to check on Tara.

Tony Mantino answered the telephone, "Ciao."

"Hello, Mr. Mantino. This is Constable McNeil speaking."

"Hello, Constable McNeil. Sergeant

Richards just phoned us. He is your friend and I want you to tell him to leave us alone!"

"May I ask what Sergeant Richards wanted?"

"He has spat upon our hospitality in the past and now he wishes to have a meeting. I told him that my answer is no—it is too late to come together."

"Mr. Mantino, I think you should have agreed to meet with Sergeant Richards."

"My wife and I are worried about Susie. Have you seen her?"

"No, I haven't seen Susan since she left the school. I'm going to hang up now and try to find her. I'll call you right back."

Freida appeared at the doorway to Kevin's office with a worried expression on her face.

Chris asked her, "Freida, did you notice anything different about Susan or did she say anything puzzling before she left the school?"

"It *was* kind of queer. Susan sort of just seemed to appear in the office. She spent a lot of time saying goodbye to several of us and then she left. I don't understand. She was crying! What's the matter?"

"Freida, I'm heading over to the district office. I'll leave my cellphone on. If you or Kevin hear from Susan, please call me."

Chris quickly telephoned the District Office and spoke to Bret Richards.

"Bret, I'm afraid Susan has gone after Bradley. I think the latest episode with Tara was too much for her. I will phone Tony Mantino to encourage him and his wife to walk over and see you at the office. I'll ask him if he will bring Tara with him. I'm on my way."

Fifteen minutes later, Mr. and Mrs. Mantino, Tara, Chris, and Bret met in the conference room at the District Office. The mood in the room was extremely strained and tension hung like a black cloud over the heads of those present. In the reception area four constables stood back against the wall casually chatting as they watched eight Mantino men all of whom were dressed in dark suits. The eight dark swarthy men sat rigidly in the visitors' chairs with expressionless faces watching the officers.

In the conference room the short powerfully built figure of Tony Mantino leaned forward as he slapped his massive fist down on the table.

"Staff Sergeant Richards, my family and I are here at the request of you and Constable McNeil. We all know where Susie is going. Now—I demand that you go across the street to Bradley's house and arrest him before our daughter gets hurt!"

"On what charge would I arrest him, Mr. Mantino? I'm more than willing to go to Mr. Bradley's house to inquire if Susan is there, but that's all I can do right now."

"Then my men and I will take care of Mr. Bradley right now."

Tony swore in Italian, rose out of his chair sending it flying across the floor and strode toward the open door. Bret Richards rapidly moved in front of the doorway.

"Mr. Mantino, taking the law into your own hands is not the solution!"

Instantly, Tony's voice rang out a command in Italian.

As his men began to vault over the counter of the reception area, one of the four officers commanded, "Halt! You can't go in there. Now get back!"

Everybody in the conference room could see Tony's men moving toward the officers. The officers stood facing them with their hands on their guns.

Chris's voice cut through the strained hush that followed, "Bret. Mr. Mantino. Please tell your men to hold up. Mr. and Mrs. Mantino, please, would you let me talk with Tara for a minute?"

Tony looked at his wife who looked pleadingly into his eyes. Then he nodded at Chris.

"Tara, would you please describe being taken down the stairs into the Black Tunnel one more time? I know you trust me. Sergeant Richards is *my* special friend and I want you to trust him. Please allow him to hear your story. Maybe we can learn something new. Please, Tara, it will help your mom. Just focus your eyes on me and tell your story."

Tara looked nervously at Bret Richards who had moved back into the room to sit at the table across from her, and then she clenched her fists. She stared into Chris's eyes as she slowly recounted the events of the Black Tunnel. Bret Richards looked at Tara and then suddenly slapped the table. Tara's face paled as she hugged her grandmother. Bret held his right hand palm up toward Tara and leaned forward.

"Tara, I'm sorry I frightened you. I guess I'm just frustrated. Twelve years ago Edgar Bradley invited me to go to his home to check out his Black Tunnel. He was mocking us. He knew we wouldn't find anything. We didn't find any green table, pictures of girls, raised platform, radios or television sets or lights in the Black Tunnel as you and your mom described."

"Sir, I told Big Chief the truth."

"I believe you, Tara. Let's try a little experiment."

"Chris, please help me move the furniture back against the wall." A few moments later, Bret muttered, "Thanks." Then he turned to Tara. "Tara, I want you to tell us again about being taken to the Black Tunnel. Keep your eyes shut and walk your way through your story. Don't worry, your grandfather, Constable McNeil and I will keep you from running into anything."

The group watched intently as Tara once again told her story. When she finished, Sergeant Bret Richards sat looking at her with a thoughtful expression on his face.

"Tara, show me once again you walking down the stairs and going into the Black Tunnel. Why did you turn right just now at the bottom of the stairs?"

"I don't know, Sergeant Richards. I thought I told you that I turned right."

"No, you didn't, but that's okay because now we have learned something new."

"Tara, imagine that you are walking from the tunnel into the room. On what side are the three doors?"

"The three doors are on my left side."

"See, we have learned another new fact. When you told us the story before, you said the doors were on the right side."

"Tara, shut your eyes and think. What was the first thing you saw when you came out on the gazebo?"

"I saw Mr. Bradley's house."

"Are you sure?"

"Yes, sir."

Bret turned and looked at the group with a thoughtful expression on his face. "Tara has just explained to us that she was in the Black Tunnel and in a room that are mirror images of those beneath Bradley's house. I'm going to phone downtown and see if I can convince a judge to issue me a search warrant for Bradley's place."

Officer Scappatura suddenly brushed by the men in the hallway and rushed into the room. She feverishly beckoned to Bret. The group sat and watched as the two officers whispered to each other. Bret shook his head and turned to face the group.

"The problem is that a search warrant will take awhile and now we don't really have the time.

Officer Scappatura just spotted Susan being forcibly taken into the Bradley house by his chauffeur. Mr. and Mrs. Mantino, I want you to keep your men here. My men are going to Bradley's place. Chris, you make sure that nobody comes after us."

"Hold on a minute!" Tony bellowed, interrupting Bret.

Bret quickly turned and shouted, "I don't understand, Mr. Mantino! My people and I need to get over to Bradley's place quickly! I happen to know that Rolf, Mr. Bradley's chauffeur, has been known to carry a gun."

"Silence!" Tony Mantino roared, thumping the table with his fist. "Sergeant Richards, *this* old mansion has a tunnel system. Mama Mia! It's the mirror image of Bradley's place! Good God! Can these tunnels be connected? I'll bet Susan is right next door to us in a hidden room!"

Tony leaped up and motioned to the others to follow him as he headed down the hall to Bret's office. Bret and the others followed him. He entered the office and dragged a chair over to the eight-foot-high dark oak bookcase behind Bret's desk. Then he stood on the chair and moved a piece of the top moulding. The bookcase silently rolled to one side, revealing a door

"Sergeant Richards, I'm sure that Susie is behind this door."

Bret walked over to the door, put his ear against it and listened for a good two minutes.

Then he looked at Chris and Charlene and whispered, "Chris, get those four constables in the hall. Tell them to bring shotguns. We'll need some backup."

Bret had everyone, with the exception of Chris and Charlene, leave the office. When the four officers arrived, Bret bent over and slowly turned the door handle. The door quietly swung open. They could hear Bradley's voice ringing forth.

"Well, Susan, I guess it's a good thing for me that Rolf here was just bringing the car around and spotted you trespassing on my land. Kind of silly of you to come here without your dad, wasn't it?"

Bret, followed by the other officers, walked slowly down a short flight of stairs and then into the dimly-lit room. His voice reverberated off the walls as he stated, "Rolf, my friend, carefully lay your gun on that table. Edgar Bradley, you are under arrest for physically assaulting Susan Mantino in 1975 and her daughter Tara Mantino in 1987."

"Sergeant Richards, you are trespassing on my land. You don't have a search warrant."

"Mr. Bradley, this land was given to the Calgary Police Service for its usage by Tony Mantino and it is still legally Mr. Mantino's land. You, sir, are the trespasser."

Edgar Bradley's eyes became panic-stricken and he seemed to look right through the officers. His face paled and he held his hands out in front of him.

Bret turned to look behind him and saw Tony Mantino with his arms around Louisa and Susan. Standing, leaning back against her grandfather, was Tara whose eyes seemed to bore into Bradley's soul. Eight Mantino men stood with arms crossed staring at Bradley and then each whispered one word in Italian. Bret turned to look back at Edgar Bradley whose hands were shaking.

Bradley screamed, "I admit my guilt on all charges! Please—arrest me! Give me protection! I will tell you everything. Just keep them away from me."

When Bret turned to look at Tony, he found that the Mantino family and their men were gone.

* * *

Two weeks later, Chief Breckenridge sat in his tenth floor corner office watching the Mantino Construction Company working on a skyscraper across from the Calgary Tower. Chris McNeil had written a letter detailing Bret Richards's fine effort in applying his investigative skills to solving the case of Edgar Bradley. Bret Richards had just laid the most surprising letter on the Chief's desk. In the letter, Bret complimented Chris McNeil on his unique talents of relating to young people and stated that those talents were valuable in bringing the case of Edgar Bradley to a successful resolution.

The Chief grinned as he slowly turned out the office lights and walked into the hall. He thought to himself that it was nice that Bret's letter indicated some growth in respect for Chris's role in District Two.

PATHWAYS

Early one spring morning, the small northwest coastal village of Ucluelet was quiet as the sun slowly began to dissolve the fog that lay upon it like a soft grey blanket. Ever so gradually, the village's mountainous sentinels revealed themselves in all their magnificent impressive splendour.

Dyana Ravyn stepped out onto the ocean-side deck of her family's rustic weather- beaten restaurant. Gazing out at the turbulent ocean, she held her arms up above her head and whispered a prayer of thanks as she greeted the dawning of the new day. She turned her head slightly and watched as her daughter, Joelle, dressed in a red-and-white jogging suit, quietly joined her. Emblazoned on the back of Joelle's jacket was a black raven—the family's symbolic tribal crest.

Joelle's long black hair tumbled over her dark eyes as she began her morning warm-up. Dyana leaned her elbows on the railing and watched as her daughter started to put her athletic body through a series of bending exercises. She grinned at Joelle.

Dyana, to the casual observer, could have been mistaken as Joelle's twin, but there were subtle differences between the two women. The mother's long dark hair had a streak of white running down each side. Her eyes were one of her most striking features. At times, they would suddenly turn red and smoulder with raw naked power. Just as quickly, the red would fade to be replaced by a deep, dark, soft texture.

Dyana was deeply respected and revered by the villagers as their grand matriarch and protector. She never seemed to change, and villagers from the youngest to the oldest could not remember a time when she had not been present offering her wise counsel to help them solve their problems. The only time that tragedy had struck the village was once when Dyana and Joelle had gone to Vancouver to visit a sick relative. While they were gone, Joelle's father had mysteriously disappeared from the village.

Finishing her warm-up, Joelle straightened up, tossed her hair back out of her eyes and grinned at her mom. "Hey you lazybones, let's go! Come running with me."

Her mother laughed. "No, Joelle. You need this time for yourself. I'll get this place in order for the Sunday morning brunch crowd while you're gone. Besides, Joelle, I foresee that today you will meet a very special man, someone from your past who will become your mate and lifelong love. You are now twenty-five and the Great Spirit has deemed that it is now time."

"Mom...sometimes I can't believe the things you say, but what's scary is...most of the time the things you say come true! Anyway, I don't have time for men right now. My place is here by your side helping you make this place a success."

"I love you with all my heart, Joelle, but it is now time for you to move on and have your own family. I am content to enjoy my friends and the people who come to our restaurant. Now, off you go and enjoy your run!"

Joelle thought to herself that life would have been so much easier if only her father hadn't disappeared. They had worked so hard to make their restaurant a success. She was happy working alongside of her mother, but now it seemed that her mom was determined that she make a life for herself. For three weeks now, Dyana had been predicting that soon Joelle would begin her life anew with a *so far non-existent* man who would supposedly become her husband.

Flipping her hair back and tying it in a ponytail, Joelle gave a wave to her mom as she vaulted off the deck and raced down the main street. Several of the young men working at the small marina paused in their labours, grinned, gave her admiring glances and waved as she headed down to the beach. Reaching the northern headland of the bay, she turned inland and raced up a densely wooded, steep, winding trail that skirted the local campground.

Eventually, the trail straightened, levelled and crossed a beautiful green meadow profusely dotted with white daisies.

All of a sudden, Joelle noticed a solitary man and his dog. The man wore a black Stetson, faded jeans and a fringed leather vest with a colourfully beaded design. He was a tall man with long dark hair. His black eyes were completely focussed on his Springer Spaniel as he guided it through a series of working-dog exercises. The man was completely unaware of Joelle's swift approach. As she neared him, she noticed with some concern a cowboy-style Winchester leaning against a massive fir tree at the edge of the meadow.

Stopping in front of him, she startled him with her sudden appearance. As he looked up, Joelle exclaimed, "Oh! Kijika! Well, hi. What are you doing here?"

"Hello. Do I know you?"

"I'm Joelle...Joelle Ravyn. We used to play together when we were kids. Don't you recognize me?"

"Joelle, you look different! You've really filled out—you're not a skinny kid anymore. I mean...you've really changed. You're all grown up. Sorry, my apologies. I'm making a complete idiot of myself."

"It's okay. Men around here have been acting funny in my presence every since my fourteenth birthday. Anyway, what are you doing up here? I noticed your rifle over there. As you know, hunting is off limits on this land."

"Don't worry, my rifle is used only for shooting at targets. This is my dog, Sheena. She and I are practicing for an exhibition that we would like to put on for the local villagers."

"Kijika, you know it might be a good idea to

explain to the Mounties and the village constables the purpose of your rifle. You might avoid any misunderstandings."

Joelle smiled, slowly sank to the ground and crossed her long legs. She held out her hand to the dog. Sheena nuzzled Joelle as she began to scratch the Springer Spaniel's neck.

"Hello, Sheena. You are a lovely clever girl."

The dog rolled over on her back. Joelle rubbed Sheena's belly while Sheena joyfully whined and her tail beat a rapid tattoo on the ground.

Slowly, Joelle stood and looked deeply into Kijika's eyes, then she smiled broadly.

"It was nice to see you, Kijika, but I guess I'd better get back to our restaurant and help my mom. Maybe we will see each other again some-time."

Kijika's eyes appeared to be focussed on the mountains in the far distance as he avoided looking directly at Joelle. Shaking her head, she turned to leave, but then Kijika quietly spoke, "Joelle, I don't want to appear to be too forward, but do you think I could come with you and maybe when you get a break you can show me around the village? I was just a young kid when I left here."

Joelle spoke in a teasing tone of voice, "Kijika means *quiet walker* not *fast runner* and I would really like to complete my run back to our restaurant. You're welcome to try and keep up with me, but if you can't, you'll see our place, *The Sea Hag*, on Main Street."

Fifteen minutes later, Dyana, who was standing on the deck, staring down the Main Street, watched as Joelle, Kijika, and Sheena raced up to her. Stopping at the bottom of the stairs leading to the deck, the three runners stared up at her. Dyana studied Kijika and Joelle's faces as she slowly walked down the stairs and then suddenly, she smiled.

She spoke to Joelle with a twinkle of amusement in her eyes. "Our family has the blood of great warriors and shaman. Few people can run as fast as you or I, but I see that you have found someone else who can!"

"Mom, I met Kijika in the meadow near the campground. Kijika, I'm sure you remember my mother, Dyana Ravyn."

To Joelle's surprise, Kijika crossed his arms over his chest and then bowed his head before Dyana. "It is my honour to meet you again, oh wise woman. Please believe me, I meant no disrespect in accompanying your daughter."

Reaching inside his vest, Kijika extracted a beautiful soapstone carving of a bird in flight and offered it to Dyana. "Oh wise woman, please accept this humble gift."

"Oh, Kijika, it's a raven— our tribal symbol! It's a beautiful piece of work and so intricate. Thank you. I accept your gift on behalf of Joelle and myself. Kijika, it was foretold that you would come here today, and therefore, there is no disrespect. You are welcome to join Joelle and me in serving the brunch crowd. Your reward for helping us will be a huge breakfast. Afterwards, I'm sure my daughter will be delighted to show you around the village."

Joelle blushed and stared down at the ground. Then, in a quizzical manner, she grinned and looked at Kijika out of the corners of her dark eyes.

Kijika stared into Dyana's eyes, which seemed to peer deeply into his soul. "It will be my honour to help you and your daughter, oh wise woman. Joelle, I would really love to have that tour around the village—if that's okay with you."

"Yes, that would be great, but Kijika, for goodness sake, please call my mother Dyana—everyone does."

Dyana moved forward and again stared into Kijika's eyes, thinking deeply.

Suddenly she frowned, her slim body stiffened and her face took on a look of deep sorrow. Joelle noticed the dramatic change in her mother, but couldn't understand the cause of it. Before she could ask her mother what was wrong, Dyana spoke, and her voice seemed to swell with power as her eyes bored into Kijika's, "KIJIKA, TELL ME ABOUT YOUR TRAVELLING COMPANION."

"How do you know that I have a travelling companion?"

"NEVER MIND, TELL ME ABOUT HIM. NOW!"

Joelle stared at her mother with a worried expression on her face. "Mom, you are frightening me! Whatever is wrong? Why are you speaking to

Kijika in that tone?"

"Joelle, please be silent," Dyana continued more calmly. "Now, Kijika, tell me about your travelling companion."

"He is simply a kindly older man that I met in Revelstoke. We decided that since we were both alone, it would be fun to travel here together. The fisherman—that is my nickname for him—said that he felt a desire to see the big island again. I told him that I also wanted to go home after sixteen years of being away. You know that I ran away from my stepfather when I was thirteen."

"Kijika, isn't it true that you have become a hero since you met that man?"

"No, I just did what had to be done."

"In Revelstoke, you helped the police find some men who had kidnapped a little girl from her motorhome in the KOA campground. Then you travelled to Hope where you again assisted the police. Some men were holding up the Royal Bank and had trapped a Mountie in his squad car with their gunfire. You came to his rescue by using your Winchester to, in turn, trap the robbers. When you caught the ferry at Tsawwassen, you discovered that a gang of American crooks was holding the captain and his officers prisoner. You and Sheena created a diversion, and then trapped the gang. These facts are all true, are they not Kijika?"

"Yes."

"Is it not also true that you have a great desire to become a famous artist?"

"Yes."

"Then it seems that you are following the wrong path in your life, does it not?"

"Dyana, I can't stand by and see people get hurt when I have the skills of a warrior to help them."

"Ah, but does it not seem strange to you that so many incidents occur that require your skills as a warrior since you met your friend?"

"Yes, I agree, it is strange."

"We will talk more of these strange things later. Kijika, did you know that your parents passed away a few years back?"

"Yes, I had heard."

"Your half-brother, Jared, is eighteen now and lives with foster parents at the south end of Main Street. Sometime back, it was discovered that on various occasions your stepfather had slipped some drugs into your mom's food and drink. The doctors said that those drugs caused Jared to be born with an uncontrollable temper. Jared has heard of your successes, and he is very jealous of you. He is getting better at coping with his problems, but maybe it would be best if you didn't see him."

"Dyana, he is my brother and the only family I have left. I must see him."

"I understand, Kijika. Joelle, take Kijika to Jared's house after we are done with the brunch crowd."

As Dyana turned to enter the restaurant, tears flowed down her cheeks. She quickly wiped her eyes with a tissue and disappeared inside. Kijika and Joelle looked at each other in surprise.

"Joelle, there is something troubling your mother. You'd better go and see what's wrong."

"No, Kijika. I have learned that my mother will eventually tell me what is the matter, but for now, she needs her privacy. Let's go in and get the tables set up."

Later that morning, Kijika, Sheena, and Joelle went to see Jared. As they neared his house, Jared stepped out of the front door.

"Joelle, I've told you many times that you are my girl! Who's this guy with you?"

"Jared, this is your brother, Kijika."

"So...this is the famous Kijika I've read about in the papers. Listen, Kijika, you may be a hero, but I won't have you stealing my girl. Now I would suggest that you leave town before you get hurt!"

"Jared, I'm not your girl!"

Kijika towered over Jared as he stepped forward and extended his hand. "Jared, I would really like to get to know my own brother. This afternoon I'm putting on a demonstration with my Winchester and my dog, Sheena. It would be great if you could come by and join us."

Jared ignored Kijika's hand and laughed. "Listen, Kijika, I don't have time to watch you show off."

* * *

Later that afternoon, Kijika and Sheena put

on their demonstration for the villagers in the same meadow where Joelle and Kijika had met. The villagers were delighted. Dyana and Joelle surprised everyone by bringing coffee, juice and cinnamon buns. After the demonstration, the people sat in the meadow and visited with Kijika. Jared surprised everyone by showing up, but he wouldn't mingle with the people, preferring to stand at the edge of the meadow and watch with a sullen look on his face. Only Dyana seemed to be able to approach him. She took him juice and a cinnamon bun. Joelle and Kijika watched as she spoke to Jared and then gave him a hug. Jared smiled and went alone to sit against a tree to eat his bun.

Dyana walked over to Kijika. "Kijika, your brother's condition makes it very hard for him to control his feelings. Please don't hate him—just try to understand him. He feels very alone. In his eyes, you have everything and he has nothing."

"Wise Mother, Jared's heart is not the only one that needs fulfillment."

"I know, Kijika, and the decisions you make in the next few days will determine whether or not you are destined to follow the pathway of a solitary warrior."

"What do you mean?"

Dyana took out the soapstone carving he had given her. She held it in her hands and stared at it as she began to speak in a soft whisper. "Kijika, the carving of the raven tells me that you are a very special man. You are a warmly compassionate being who has given life to the cold stone and shaped this work of art. It is, indeed, special. You seek to please the one you perceive to be your friend by willingly serving as his weapon against evil, and by doing so, *you risk* losing your ability to feel, to show compassion, and to love. You must decide who you are. My daughter loves you, but she, like me, loves the total you—not just the warrior."

Joelle stared at her mother and then at Kijika. "*Mother*, pleas*e*, you are embarrassing Kijika and me."

Dyana slowly walked away, leaving Kijika and Joelle to ponder her words.

Suddenly, Kijika noticed his travelling companion standing on the trail. As he and Joelle continued to watch Dyana, they saw her turn and walk purposely over to the tall, gaunt man. To their surprise, Dyana embraced the grey-bearded man. When she walked away, there were tears in her eyes. The young couple watched as she disappeared down the trail to the ocean.

Joelle studied the man, gasped in surprise, then turned to look at Kijika. "Kijika, I know that man! He is someone I lost a long time ago. The beard and long hair have changed his appearance, but I know that man."

"Joelle, that is my travelling companion, Elso."

"That is my father! I must go to my mother."

Kijika watched as Joelle raced down the trail toward the ocean. As she approached the man, she paused and gazed into his eyes. The man bowed his head and stared down at the ground. Joelle brought a hand to her face, wiped her eyes and then hurried on down the trail.

Over the next several days, Kijika and Joelle could be seen throughout the village walking hand in hand and smiling. The couple would sit for hours in the beautiful meadow where they had met, while Sheena dozed at their feet or chased the butterflies. Kijika carved various little animals from soapstone for Joelle. Elso would always show up in the middle of the afternoon and insist that it was time for Kijika to practice his marksmanship. Never once did Joelle say a word to her father. She would walk over to him, look tearfully into his eyes, then give him a hug and disappear down the oceanside trail.

Jared could often be seen watching the happy couple from a distance. One day, he confronted Kijika and threatened him. The much larger Kijika firmly, but gently, told him to leave. Jared grabbed Kijika by the shirt and tried to hit him. Kijika easily blocked the blow and bodily picked up Jared. He placed him in his truck and drove him home.

* * *

Early the next morning, fog enveloped the little village. It was before sunrise and Dyana had gone down to the docks to meet a fishing boat that was bringing in supplies for the restaurant.

Stealthily, Jared entered *The Sea Hag* through the back door. He caught Joelle in the kitchen. Threatening her with a 9-millimetre Beretta pistol that he had stolen from his foster father, he fired a shot into the air. Meanwhile back at the campground, Elso *knew* that Joelle was in trouble at the restaurant. He told Kijika and immediately, Kijika and Sheena raced out of the campground, through the meadow, down the oceanside trail and up onto the main street of the little village.

Arriving in front of the restaurant, Kijika and Sheena quietly moved like phantoms in the night as they climbed onto the deck. They crept into the dimly-lit restaurant. Firmly gripped in Kijika's left hand was his cowboy-style Winchester. He studied the scene that met his eyes, noting the light that seeped out under the closed kitchen door. Quietly, he tipped over several tables.

Then, he whispered to Sheena, "Sheena, tell Joelle that we are here."

The Springer Spaniel barked three times. Then Kijika signalled for Sheena to go behind the table on his left hand side. Light poured through the doorway and two shadowy silhouettes could be seen. The light of the kitchen glowed behind them and cast elongated shadows across the restaurant's floor. Kijika's eyes narrowed as he felt his anger rise. Quickly, he reached over to the left with his free hand and turned on the restaurant's lights. He stared into Jared's cold grey eyes. Jared's left arm encircled Joelle's waist as he held her firmly in front of him. Strangely, Joelle's eyes displayed sorrow not fear as she looked at Kijika and then back into Jared's eyes. Jared's right hand held the pistol that he aimed menacingly at Kijika. The Springer Spaniel laid her ears back, tensed her body and waited for Kijika's next hand signal.

Jared laughed. His voice echoed off the walls and seemed to fill the eerie silence of the restaurant. "Well, my dear brother, now Joelle's going to find out whether or not you're a *real* man!"

"Come on, Jared. Let Joelle go!"

"Why should I?"

"Jared, you're threatening a person I care very deeply about. Now, lay the gun down!"

Tears filled Joelle's eyes as she whispered, "Oh, Kijika."

Kijika, in spite of the gravity of the situation, blushed and quietly mouthed the words, "Well, I do."

Jared screamed, "No, Kijika! If I can't have a girlfriend, then neither can you!"

"Jared, that's crazy! It's your condition that's making you overreact to everything."

"I don't have a condition. So what if mom was drugged before I was born—what the heck does that have to do with anything? Now I want you to leave!"

"No, Jared."

"Get out of here or I will shoot you both!"

"No!"

Jared raised his pistol and aimed it at Kijika. Kijika secretly signalled with his right hand for

Sheena to leap at Jared, but strangely, the Springer Spaniel had disappeared from behind her table.

Just then, Joelle drove her elbow hard into Jared's stomach and twisted away from him. She swiftly turned and stood between the two men. Holding out her hands toward Jared, she spoke to him in a calm soothing tone.

"Jared, please stop this or you're going to die."

"Fat chance, Joelle! My brother will never shoot as long as you're between the two of us. Obviously that rifle is just for show. Good old Kijika doesn't have the guts to shoot anybody or anything, but I do!"

"Jared, it's not Kijika that you should fear. I sense that my mother is coming."

"Don't be ridiculous, Dyana wouldn't hurt me. She is a gentle spirit and she'll protect me."

"Oh, Jared, don't you understand? You have threatened me, Dyana's daughter. She is very angry. Listen to the thunder and see the lightning."

Just then, a bolt of lightning struck the ground outside the window of the restaurant and thunder rattled the building. Suddenly, Joelle dove behind an overturned table and Jared found himself staring into the barrel of Kijika's Winchester. Jared started to squeeze the trigger of his pistol, but Kijika was no longer in front of him, but to his right side. Quickly, he swung his gun toward Kijika. A blood-curdling growl echoed through the restaurant as Sheena leaped through the air onto Jared's back. Jared crashed to the floor and rolled over. His arm swung around and he accidentally hit Sheena on the side of her head with his gun. The Springer Spaniel collapsed in a heap. Jared slowly climbed back up to his feet. Fear mounted in his heart as he stared into Kijika's icy cold eyes.

Kijika's voice took on a steely tone as he growled, "Jared, you have threatened the woman I love, and hurt the only friend that I ever had through the lonely years of my wanderings."

Just then, Dyana's image appeared behind Jared. Her voice filled Kijika's mind as she cried, "Kijika! For your and Joelle's future think about what action you should take! Are you Kijika—the unbridled, cold ruthless warrior, or are you Kijika—the man who tempers his actions with love and compassion?"

The Winchester spat out its litany of death. Jared screamed as he felt the pistol fly out of his right hand and bullets whistle by his body. Shaking, he sank to his knees, eyes fixating on the floor, his arms dangling at his sides. Kijika turned, dropped his rifle on the floor, and walked slowly out of the restaurant.

Later, the police having had gunshot sounds reported to them cautiously entered *The Sea Hag* to find Joelle and Dyana tenderly placing Jared in a chair. Dyana explained to the police that Jared's condition had caused him to have a seizure and that he badly needed to be taken home for some bedrest. *The police found no evidence of any guns or that any guns had been fired.*

The women next turned their attention to

the unconscious Sheena. Dyana placed her hands on Sheena's wound, and it miraculously began to heal.

Dyana hugged Sheena close to her as she spoke. "Oh, Sheena, please forgive me. I am so sorry that you were hurt, but there was nothing I could do. It was important that Kijika find his own path."

Joelle stared at her mother. "Mom, could you have stopped what happened, but chose not to?"

"Yes."

"Why?"

"Joelle, *we* are beings of infinite power, but it is important that we allow others to find their own way. Kijika will never realize his full potential unless he is forced to examine the path that he has been set upon."

"Set upon by whom? Oh no! Dad! He *is* going to take away my love and soulmate, isn't he? Why would he do such a thing?"

"Joelle, your father is a noble being who sees in Kijika an opportunity to battle evil. I, myself, advise and suggest *pathways* to others. Let us just say that your father is more direct in his methods."

"But he sent Kijika to kill his own brother!"

"No, Joelle. He sent Kijika to save his daughter. It was Kijika's decision as to how he saved you."

"But Mom, what of Kijika's and my life together? What is to become of us? It is not fair that Kijika be doomed to wander the world as less a person than he could be."

"Ah, Joelle, now it is time you stopped being less than you are! Exert your power to the fullest and confront your father. Make him understand that Kijika is your love and you belong together. Fight for him, Joelle! Remember that love is the strongest power in the universe. Kijika will be coming back to *The Sea Hag*. After that, you must go and see your father."

* * *

Later that evening, bands of fog stretched over the village. Only the twin points of land at the ends of the crescent-shaped bay were visible. It seemed that a titanic struggle was imminent. The outcome of that struggle would have a permanent effect on Kijika and perhaps others.

High up on the cliff behind Ucluelet, Kijika stood staring down at the thunderous waves that dashed against the shore sending foam cascading up the rocks. With tears in his eyes, he turned to look down at his beloved village for what he believed to be the last time.

Eventually, he began walking down the narrow path that meandered its way into the small coastal village. Five minutes later, he entered the village and walked slowly along the short main street. Focussing on the headland at the north end of town, Kijika thought about what had happened to Sheena and Jared. Finally, he stopped in front of

The Sea Hag and quietly climbed the stairs onto the front deck. He stared through the large window and caught sight of Joelle helping her mother set the tables. Tears rolled down his cheeks as he watched the two women smile at each other. He had just turned to leave, when behind him Joelle's voice quietly filled the silence.

"Are you okay? You look very tired, Kijika."

"No, I'm not okay. My brother will never be normal again. And now Sheena is hurt, maybe dying. Sheena who helped me through all the bad times."

"Jared has never acted normally—you didn't cause his condition."

"Joelle, I have special talents which set me apart from others. I will always be alone and lonely."

"Oh, Kijika, the isolation—the loneliness that you feel—it is within yourself. We have each other. You are my beloved and my soulmate!"

"You know how I feel about you."

"Yes, I do, but tell me again."

"Joelle, I love you!"

"Kijika, look who's here!"

Sheena rushed past Joelle and leaped up into Kijika's arms. She started to lick his face as Kijika's mouth broadened into a wide grin. "Sheena—I thought you were dying!"

"My mother saved her."

"How did she do that?"

"Mom used *her hands* to heal Sheena."

"Dyana has mysterious powers."

"Kijika, I can do the same things as my mother. Does that worry you?"

"No. But Joelle, I've got to go now. I've been called to meet your father—he's waiting for me at the meadow. I think he wants us to move on and help other people. I love you, Joelle! Will you please keep Sheena with you? I wish things could have been different."

Joelle watched tearfully as Kijika walked away from her and down toward the beach. Sheena looked up at her and whined. Then Dyana appeared from the shadows of the restaurant. She walked up to Joelle and gently placed her hand on her daughter's shoulder.

"Go after him, Joelle, or you will lose him."

"Dad has a powerful hold over Kijika, Mom. I don't know how to fight him. I have already lost Kijika's love."

"No, you haven't! Think about whom Kijika loves. Go to him!"

As Kijika walked down the deserted beach, he was lost in thought. Usually he would have been accompanied by Sheena who would have delighted in running at top speed back and forth to her master. Kijika thought about the many joyous times that he had enjoyed with Sheena and Joelle on the beach. Smiling, he thought about when he had first returned to Ucluelet and how he had met the lovely, dark-haired Joelle in the meadow, their favourite place. They had become inseparable. Now, he walked *alone* up the trail to the meadow where he and Joelle had spent so many happy hours. As he reached the meadow, Kijika saw Elso. Elso, his grey hair rippling in the wind, motioned for Kijika to join him.

"Kijika, I have hitched up the fifth wheel to the truck. We are ready to go. I sense that we will be needed in Victoria."

"Where does it all end, Elso?"

"What do you mean?"

"I don't understand you, Elso. You have a beautiful wife and daughter, yet you would have us running all around the countryside dealing with crisis after crisis. Don't you ever just want to be with Dyana and Joelle?"

Elso frowned and ignored Kijika's question.

"Kijika, there is evil loose in this land. I have groomed you to deal with that evil. Does it not give you satisfaction— a purpose in dealing with that evil? Before you met me you had no purpose, but now you are a force for good."

Suddenly, there was a crack of thunder that rolled up the valley. A column of light formed in the centre of the meadow. As the light faded, three shapes were revealed—Joelle, Jared and Sheena.

Joelle stared at her father and then spoke in measured tones, "Dad, you have used Kijika for your own purposes. He is much more than a living weapon. He is a warm, loving, compassionate being who deserves to live his life to the fullest."

Joelle removed several soapstone carvings from her jacket and laid them on the ground at her father's feet.

"Look, Dad, at Kijika's work. Look at how he has given life to the soapstone. Look at how Sheena comes to him and willingly does his bidding because of their special bond, not out of fear. Jared, you have something to say to my father."

"Mr. Elso, I still think that Kijika is just a show-off. But even when I threatened his girl, he was still kind to me. I thought that only Dyana and Joelle were kind. He's my brother, Mr. Elso, and I sure as heck won't let you take him away!"

Joelle smiled and gently placed her hand on Jared's shoulder. "Jared, stay calm. Kijika, you must decide between going with my father or staying with us. What is your decision?"

Kijika smiled and held out his hands to Joelle and Jared. Sheena barked and ran around in circles. The foursome started to walk away.

Elso raised his arms. His voice thundered as he screamed, "Stop!"

A burst of light forked down from the sky toward the group. Joelle held up her hand and the light deflected away.

"You can't hurt us, Dad. We are protected by our love."

Joelle and the others disappeared down the oceanside trail to the beach below.

Elso smiled as he quickly looked up and caught sight of a figure with long black hair, that had two white streaks in it, disappearing into the woods.

He quietly said to himself, "It is not your love for Kijika that protects you, Joelle, but a mother's love for her daughter. But, then again, I would not have let anything happen to you or your friends. It was simply a test of your love for Kijika and you have done well. I am very proud of you, my daughter."

That evening as the wind howled furiously around the north headland of the bay, two figures stood on the top of the cliff in the midst of a pocket of calm. They stared deeply into each other's eyes and then, both smiled.

Elso spoke in chiding tones, "Dyana, you have once again had the audacity to interfere with my work to stem the tide of evil. By taking Kijika away from me, you put our daughter's happiness foremost."

"And you, my dear husband, once again chose to manipulate others to your own purposes. By making Kijika your tool, you had taken away his free will and any chance he had to live his life to the fullest. The creator gave man free will. It is our responsibility to allow others a choice. The most we should do, is to provide advice when called upon."

"But, did you not interfere directly in Kijika's life by getting him to stay with Joelle?"

"No, the love that he has for Joelle controls his heart and actions. I don't control him. The love that Joelle and Kijika have for each other is the force that will determine their future."

Elso smiled to himself, still remembering Dyana's appearance at the meadow, but decided it was better to keep that knowledge to himself forever.

"What then is our role in this world, dearly beloved Dyana? What is there left for us? What is our purpose?"

"Well, my love, husband and sometimes nemesis, Joelle and Kijika will soon be married and then I will be alone. Running a restaurant by myself can be a lonely task. Perhaps it is time you stopped wandering around the countryside and settled down."

"It is tempting, Dyana, but to stop completely having a role in the affairs of the world seems so mundane."

"Ah, but in a village restaurant you get to listen to the tales of woe and joy of the people. Invariably they will expect you to dispense with advice and, of course, be sympathetic."

Elso stood at the edge of the cliff staring down into the water. He pondered the ebb and flow of the great majestic turbulent ocean.

Then he turned, smiled and extended his hand to Dyana. She grinned back and opened her arms wide to him. Elso knew that he had finally come home, and like Kijika, he would wander no more. It was time to enjoy the peace, love and happiness of his family.

Joelle and Kijika stood on the front deck of the restaurant staring up toward the two figures, standing on the cliffs, and watched as the radiance of love lit up the sky. Joelle smiled, placed her hand in Kijika's, and led him inside the restaurant.

*   *   *

And four beings had come together,
And their lives had become intertwined
Through their love,
And thus, they would, for evermore
Share their pathways of life.

THE KINDRED SPIRIT

In the 1960's Philip Ashcroft, Calgary born billionaire, was reputed to be a great philanthropist. He was highly respected as a self-made man, short on words, and long on actions. Seeing that the government needed a building in Calgary to house Social Workers, he immediately, in an apparently completely unselfish act, loaned them the usage of one of his mansions. A local newspaper reported that this act of benevolence was just another fine example of Mr. Ashcroft's completely unfettered love for his community and fellow man.

The mansion had, of course, many rooms, but one in particular had a unique feature. The room's oak walls sported intricately-carved scenes of the Leduc and Turner Valley Oil Fields, offering overwhelming evidence that in past times Mr. Ashcroft and his cronies in the petroleum business had used it for many an eloquent affair to celebrate their newly-acquired riches. Social Workers involved in adoptions now met in the room with couples who were hoping that they would be chosen worthy to be new parents.

On one particular sunny spring morning, a young couple sat waiting at the long oak table that dominated the centre of the room. They knew their Social Worker would have already determined whether or not their dream of welcoming a baby into their home would become reality—a baby girl they planned to name Kathy.

Nate's huge right hand gently caressed Julia's as his keen eyes examined every minute detail of the room. His slate gray eyes and the firm set of his mouth portrayed displeasure as he whirled to glare at his wife.

In a low base voice laced with anger, Nate growled, "These government bureaucrats are unbelievable in their demands!"

Rising quickly from his leather seat, he snatched up his black Stetson, plopped it on his head, and then turned toward the door. Julia's large dark eyes momentarily displayed shocked surprise, and then she vigorously shook her head. Her eyes looked beseechingly at her husband as she, to his surprise, grasped his arm with a strength that belied her petite size and firmly pulled him down.

"Please, love, don't leave! We have come here to become parents. Mrs. Arkins said they have a precious little baby for us—a daughter for us to love and cherish, Nate. According to Mrs. Arkins, the baby is blonde, pretty, and well, just perfect in every way. Think of all the things that we can teach her and places where we can take her and just share with her. Nate, we will be a family and someday she will call us mommy and daddy."

Nate slowly took his wife's hands in his and stared into her tear-filled eyes. He thought of the many reasons why he deeply loved her. Perhaps the bedrock of their marriage was centred on their complete and utter devotion to one another as well as the endless support they gave each other.

Nate crossed his arms over his barrel chest, then glared at the mirrors in the room. "Julia, I don't know what's going on here, but we are being observed like common criminals. Don't look at me that way! I'm not being paranoid! I'm sure that the baby is special, but I for one will not be treated this way. Now come on, let's get out of here! Let's go back to the ranch where at least people are straightforward and honest. If we are acceptable parents, then the government bureaucrats don't have to sneak around behind one-way mirrors spying on us."

Julia vigorously shook her head again. "No, Nate. We are staying! Listen, I want you to stay put in that chair and cooperate. I love you dearly, but if you get up again, I'm going to—well, I don't know what I will do, but I'll do something. Okay?"

A look of admonishment appeared in Julia's black eyes as she sat glaring at her husband. Nate studiously tried to ignore Julia's eyes. He hunched his massive shoulders as he leaned forward and riveted his eyes on one of the largest mirrors in the room.

"Julia, I really do want to be here. Nothing is more important to me than your happiness, but I don't want to toady up to some institutionalized government bureaucrat just so that that Social Worker, Mrs. Arkins, might just decide to give us an opportunity to be parents. Between the two of us, we have an infinite well of love, caring and knowledge to offer Kathy—I mean the baby girl. You would make a wonderful mother, and I would like to think that I have something to offer little Kathy, but here we sit playing some kind of fool game!"

Nate Racine leaned forward on his elbows, grasped his large powerful hands together and then slumped back into his seat. He began nervously to make circular motions with his thumbs. Julia thoughtfully watched her husband for a few long moments, then leaned over and gently kissed him on the cheek.

Laying her head on Nate's shoulder, she whispered, "Nate, I love you. It's all right. I want her to be our Kathy too, but don't you think it's best that we sit and wait?"

Nate reached out his hand engulfing Julia's in his then smiled as he stared into her eyes. He gently touched a finger to her trembling lower lip and whispered, "Okay, Julia."

A door handle turned and the door burst open. Phyllis Arkins stepped into the room, then kicked backwards causing the door to slam shut. Hands clutching a stack of files, she scurried into the room. Her close-cropped pageboy haircut appeared to have two horns emanating near the proximity of her ears, but they were in reality two red pens. She attempted, but failed to maintain a professionally courteous smile as nervously glancing through the corners of her eyes at Nate and

Julia, she dropped the files on the table with a resounding thud. Vigorously shaking hands with Julia, the Social Worker kept glancing at Nate, and then stared at the floor as she shook hands with him. Sitting down across from Nate and Julia, she fished through the pile of folders and picked up one.

For a few long moments Phyllis focussed thoughtfully on the file folder then, she looked at Julia and Nate.

"I'm sorry I'm late. When I discovered that I was behind schedule, which is not unusual for me, I hopped right on over."

Nate's eyes were initially steely as he stared at Phyllis, then a small fleeting smile appeared on his lips and for a few seconds his eyes twinkled in amusement. Just as quickly the smile disappeared. Nate's facial features hardened, and he locked eyes with Phyllis who quickly looked back down at the floor.

Smiling as she leaned forward, chin resting on her hand, Julia said, "We *are* being observed. Isn't that right, Mrs. Arkins?"

"Yes, you are being watched, Julia."

"Please tell us who is behind that glass."

"I'm afraid, Julia, I can't do that."

"What do you mean you can't tell us?" Nate spoke slowly in measured, controlled tones. "Mrs. Arkins, tell us who is behind that glass or I will call my lawyer, Peter Jenkins, right now."

'Peter Jenkins is the senior partner of the law firm, Jenkins, Doherty, and Johnson. He's worked with Social Services on many an occasion

to fine-tune the adoption procedures and other aspects of the Child Welfare Act. Five seconds would be all it would take for him to recognize the illegality of the present situation. It may cost me my job, but I had better come clean,' Phyllis thought to herself.

"My supervisor, Mrs. Lydia Austin, and a child psychiatrist from the Children's Hospital, Dr. Maureen Randham, are in the next room," Phyllis stated in an expressionless voice.

Nate leaned forward on his elbows as his deep voice rumbled, "Mrs. Arkins, tell Mrs. Austin and Mo to come in here or Julia and I will leave right now."

Phyllis replied in a perplexed tone, "Mo?"

Nate just sat back and smiled.

The door opened and two women walked into the room. They each sat down at the end of the table and looked at Nate.

"All right, Mo, why are you and Mrs. Austin spying on us?" Nate demanded in a loud voice.

"Nate, Lydia and I are very concerned that this baby be adopted by a very loving couple. She's coming from a terrible accident."

"What sort of an accident?"

"It was a car accident, Nate. The father was killed outright and the mother will never walk again. She wanted her baby to be adopted by a loving couple and has signed all the necessary papers."

"Has the baby been injured, Mrs. Arkins?"

"No, Julia. The baby is physically perfect.

The deceased father's name is Ethan. He was an honours law student at the University of Calgary. His family was made up of several generations of distinguished people in the petroleum industry. The mother's name is Tessa. She is or was an honours arts student. Her father worked as a postal worker and her mother took in jobs at home as a seamstress. Tessa was pursuing a career in live theatre as a dancer and singer."

"Mrs. Arkins, I don't understand. Why don't their families take the baby?"

"Well …apparently the families disapproved so strongly of the marriage that they completely cut them out of their lives and now refuse to acknowledge any familial ties."

Julia shook her head in anger. "I'll never understand how parents can disown their children or how they can let an innocent baby—their own grandchild—be adopted by strangers."

"Julia, the reason that Dr. Randham and Mrs. Austin are assisting me is due to the nature of this adoption." Phyllis sat back in her chair and looked at Nate and Julia.

Mo smiled at Nate and said, "Nate, I didn't know that you and Julia were the intended parents for this little baby." Turning to look at Lydia she continued, "My recommendation is that the adoption proceed as Julia and Nate are, in my opinion, perfect choices. Lydia, my old friend Nate left the university to become an independent consultant in the fields of Physics, Mathematics, and Structural Engineering. He is part of the same think tank as I am and is, in essence, a brilliant man. Nate is one of the most compassionate and loving men I've ever known. Julia is a première dancer and singer and could have gone to the United States to become a big name; however, like Nate, she is very independent and has her own studio at their ranch where she teaches in her specialty areas. However, Phyllis and Lydia, I'm sure that you know all these facts. Lydia, do you have any comments?"

"Yes, I do. First, Mr. Racine, I do not appreciate your comments about government employees. However, given the situation I suppose I would be upset the same as you. I think that the talents that you and Julia have will give this baby the balanced personality needed to deal with any challenges that life throws her way."

Without another word Mo and Lydia rose from their chairs. They shook hands with Nate and Julia, smiled at Phyllis, and then started out of the room. Mo gave Nate and Julia a little wave and a slight smile as she went out.

"Lydia will be bringing the baby in, in a few minutes," Phyllis said to the couple.

Five minutes later, the door opened and Lydia walked in with a beautiful little baby girl in her arms. "Mr. Racine, I hope I'm right in saying, *Dad, say hello to your new daughter.*"

Nate sat there with tears in his eyes and held out his arms. "Thank you, Mrs. Austin," Nate mumbled.

Julia smiled as she cooed over the baby. "Well, hello little one. Are you going to come home with us and be our little Kathy?"

Phyllis got out of her chair as she said, "Maybe I should leave the three of you alone."

"No, Mrs. Arkins. This is our Kathy. We want to take her home now." Julia stared up at Phyllis who smiled and nodded her head.

Later, Lydia Austin walked down a secret hallway that skirted the room until she reached a doorway where she paused and knocked twice.

A man's voice quietly called, "Come in."

Lydia stared at the back of the man's head with hatred in her eyes. "It's done."

"I observed everything that you and your worker did. I'm satisfied. Now the last order that you are to carry out for me and in accordance with my friend, the Minister of Social Welfare, and your boss, is to have the little girl's records sealed in an underground government vault." Phillip Ashcroft turned and glared at Lydia Austin with his steel blue eyes.

"Yes, sir." Lydia turned slowly and walked out of the room.

* * *

Thirty-five years later, Kathy porched on a bench seat dressed in her matching red shorts, halter-top, and headband and gazed downward through one of the dormers of her ranch-house loft. The loft served as a dance studio for her and her friend, Chrissy. Both ladies enjoyed teaching dance classes. Using a towel to wipe the sweat from her face and upper torso, Kathy watched as the last student of the day ran out to her parent's truck and waved at her with great gusto. The silver-gray, metallic-coloured truck lurched forward and then was gone in a cloud of dust down the gravelled section road. Turning her attention in the direction of the town of Cochrane, a broad smile appeared on Kathy's face as she saw a tiny yellow speck in the far distance approaching on the road that ran by the ranch she shared with her husband, Danny.

"Come on, Chrissy. The school bus will be here in a few minutes. Let's go downstairs and put out some milk and chocolate chip cookies for our girls."

Chrissy, dressed in a purple outfit identical to Kathy's, laughed as she quickly finished sorting the sheet music, tapes, and CDs into neat piles on top of the piano. *'Cindy and Rochelle are home,'* she thought to herself. Jumping up from the piano, she followed Kathy down to the spacious kitchen.

The school bus carrying the girls stopped in front of the house in a swirling cloud of dust. Kathy and Chrissy literally flew around the room putting on a pot of coffee, taking out a jug of milk, cream, sugar, mugs, glasses, and a plate full of homemade cookies. They placed everything on the table just as Cindy and Rochelle came bounding into the kitchen. Tossing their knapsacks into a corner, they walked over to Kathy and Chrissy and gave them each a big hug. Rochelle and Chrissy went over to the table and sat down, but Cindy stayed standing, her arms tightly wrapped around her mother. Kathy ran her fingers through her daughter's long blonde hair then rubbed her back feeling the tension in her daughter's muscles. She looked over Cindy's head at Chrissy with a puzzled look. After a few long moments, Kathy stepped back to look at Cindy and was startled to see tears flowing down her daughter's angelic face. Giving Cindy some tissues, Kathy took her daughter by the hand and walked over to the kitchen table to join Chrissy and Rochelle.

After a few minutes of silence, Kathy said, "Cindy, do you want to talk about it?"

"No, Mom. Well…I guess so. It's just that Mr. Stapleton, our English teacher, is such a doofus." Cindy shook her head, bit down on a cookie and took a big swig of milk.

"Mr. Stapleton is a what? I thought you told me that all the kids thought he was great."

Cindy looked down at the table. "Well, Mr. Stapleton usually is great, but you should see the latest assignment he gave us." Cindy leaned back in her chair, crossed her arms and looked angrily out of the kitchen window.

At that moment the back door was flung open. Two large men in dirty old Stetsons and dusty, ragged jeans appeared in the doorway. Danny Thompson, Kathy's husband, and Joel Stewart, Chrissy's husband, dropped their tool belts on the back landing as they trudged into the kitchen and headed for the fridge. Kathy leaped off her chair and ran around in front of them. She held up her hands to stop them.

"All right, you two. I want you to wash up before you put your hands on anything in my kitchen. There's the sink," Kathy firmly stated. "I've made coffee for you or you can have some cold soft drinks."

"Well, can I at least have a kiss?" Danny smiled mischievously at Kathy.

"Hey, Chrissy. We've been working on the fences all day and deserve some personal attention," Joel said as he walked over to the table and held out his arms to his wife. She playfully shook her head.

"Joel, you heard Kathy."

Rochelle stood up with a big grin on her face and put a hand on her hip. "People, you're disturbing us. Settle down here. Honestly, some people's parents have to learn to act their age!"

"Taskmasters," Danny muttered with a smile as he marched over to the sink. He glanced over at the girls and motioned to Kathy. He had noticed Cindy's tear-stained cheeks and he whispered, "Kathy, what's wrong with Cindy?"

"I don't know yet, Danny. It's something about an assignment that her teacher gave the class. I was just on the brink of talking to her when you came in." Kathy turned around and walked over to the table to sit down beside Cindy.

After the men had finished washing up, they sat down at the table with their wives and daughters. Kathy reached over to put her hand on Cindy's arm and smiled at her. "Cindy, I would like to see the assignment from Mr. Stapleton."

"Mom, there's no point in looking at it. I

just can't do it. Besides, it will upset you."

"Sweetheart, I won't get upset. I would just like to see the assignment."

"Cindy, do as your mother says." Danny's deep voice rumbled as he looked at Cindy.

Cindy got out of her chair and went over to her knapsack. She extracted a single sheet of paper and brought it to Kathy, who carefully read it. Shaking her head she passed it to Danny, who scanned it.

"I guess you can do the assignment on your father's side of the family, sweetheart. I'm sorry, but according to Mr. Stapleton's directions the family tree is to be of people who are your ancestors by birth or bloodlines. As you know, Grandma Julia and Grandpa Nate adopted me when I was a baby. I think the only thing you can do is trace your dad's family."

"But Mom, that's not fair! Grandma and grandpa *are* my grandparents. Grandma Julia is always over here helping you with our dancing. Boy, grandma is really something special when she starts moving and grooving on the dance floor. And you know Grandpa Nate is so cool the way he helps Rochelle and me with our math problems. Some people say girls are supposed to hate Math and Science, but you know he makes it so interesting. Rochelle and I wouldn't be getting top marks if it weren't for Grandpa Nate." Pausing, Cindy first looked into Danny's eyes, then Joel's. She quickly added, "Dad and Mr. Stewart, you help us too, but it's just that...grandpa is kind of special in those areas. And besides, I don't want to make my family tree if I can't put them in it."

Danny gently ruffled Cindy's hair. "It's okay, sweetheart. Nate and Julia are two of the most talented, loving, sharing grandparents that a granddaughter could ever wish for. I remember after we were married how generous Nate and Julia were in helping your mom and me get settled out here at the ranch. Soon after that Nate and Julia moved into their house in Cochrane, but whenever we've needed some help or advice they have been here for us." Danny stopped talking and stared out of the kitchen window for a few minutes, then looked at Kathy. "Kathy, I think one of us should give Mr. Stapleton a call."

Kathy nodded her head and said, "Okay, I'll do it. Maybe Mr. Stapleton will modify the assignment to allow relatives by adoption. Chrissy, you were adopted. Do you want me to ask the teacher to do the same for Rochelle?"

Chrissy and Joel glanced at each other. "No, Kathy, that won't be necessary," Chrissy said in a quiet nervous voice.

"But Chrissy, Rochelle won't be able to do this assignment."

"Yes she will, Kathy. I've got something I have to tell you. I didn't say anything in the beginning because I was afraid it wouldn't amount to much, but I have been secretly trying to find my birth parents for the past two years. Honestly, I was going to tell you what I have been up to. You see when we were away for a few days last week a very special thing happened. Kathy…I found my birth mom! I know I should have told you all right away." Chrissy looked over at Rochelle, who was sitting there with eyes as round as saucers, and then glanced back at Kathy as she continued. "But, I needed time to hug the news to myself. Anyway, last week Joel and I flew out to British Columbia to meet my birth mother and her husband." Turning back to look at Rochelle, Chrissy continued, "Rochelle, dad and I are planning to take you with us next time so that you can meet my birth mom. She especially asked us to bring you."

"Mom, I think that'll be terrific! Do you and your birth mom look alike? Does she have any other kids? What should I wear?" Rochelle had moved off her chair and was standing beside Chrissy as she started to ask her mom question after question.

Joel leaned over and gently touched Rochelle's arm. "Sweetheart, your mom and I will sit and talk to you when we get home. Okay?"

"Okay, Dad." Joel gave Rochelle a hug and she sat back down.

Cindy suddenly stood up and angrily glared at everyone. Quickly Danny said, "Kathy, you'd better phone the teacher before he goes home."

Reluctantly, Kathy left the table and made the phone call to the school. The teacher told Kathy he was sorry that he hadn't included adoptive relatives as part of the family tree, that it was an oversight, and to tell Cindy to go ahead and do her family tree.

Hanging up the telephone, Kathy walked back to the table. "You can include Grandma Julia and Grandpa Nate in your family tree, she reported quietly." Slowly sitting down, she looked questioningly at Chrissy. "We've been friends ever since Elementary School, Chrissy. How come you didn't tell me?"

Chrissy reached over and grasped Joel's right hand, then looked beseechingly into Kathy's hurt eyes. "Because...I don't know, Kathy. It seemed like the more searching that I did, the more I wanted to keep it private. Joel and I felt that it was just something I needed to do for myself. Kathy, I love you and I'm sorry if I hurt your feelings." Chrissy turned her head as a couple of tears trickled over her cheeks.

Danny reached across the table to take Kathy's hand. "Honey, I think you and I are so very lucky to have friends like Joel and Chrissy, but you know there are times when only a husband and wife should share certain things. We have certainly gone through times like that. Remember when you lost the baby? It was a long time before we could even bring ourselves to talk to anyone about anything relating to our son's death. I'm sure that Chrissy will tell us whatever she feels comfortable sharing with us."

Joel pointed at the door and said to Chrissy, "Go upstairs, dear, and get changed. You and Kathy go and have a good walk. Rochelle and I will meet you at home. Don't worry about supper. Tonight I'll barbecue."

Chrissy leaned over Joel and gave him a kiss. "Thank you, dear."

Fifteen minutes later, Chrissy and Kathy met at the front door of the ranch house and went walking.

Chrissy looked at Kathy. "Kathy, there is not much to tell you right now. Usually people find each other through the registry or some other governmental service. I had tried that, but didn't get anywhere. Luckily, I decided to place an ad in all of the small town newspapers in British Columbia. My birth mother saw the ad and called me. She wanted to know if I'd had a good home and if my parents had loved me. She was anxious to meet me. I was excited, but I was so nervous, Kathy. Anyway, Joel and I flew out to meet her. She is a very nice lady and she made me feel very welcome. She said she would love to meet her new granddaughter. Anyway, I could see all the past hurt in her eyes. She told me she would tell me all about our past, but for right now, could we all just get to know each other." Chrissy stopped talking and there was silence.

The two friends trudged on along beside a creek for a few minutes. Finally Kathy spoke. "Chrissy, I'm sorry. It's just that...well, we're such close friends and I guess I felt a little hurt that you hadn't shared your searching with me and...well, I guess I'm envious of you too. I'm sorry, here I am going on feeling sorry for myself and honestly, Chrissy, I really am happy for you. It's so exciting!"

The two friends looked at each other and came together in a hug.

"You know, Kathy, maybe you should search for your roots too."

*   *   *

One day, about six months later, Danny arrived home from Calgary. It was Thursday, so he knew that Kathy and Chrissy wouldn't have any dance students. The thought of having Kathy home alone for a change brought a big mischievous smile to Danny's rugged face. He slipped off his cowboy boots at the front door, and quietly sneaked up to the loft where he hoped to surprise his beautiful wife. As he rounded the corner into the loft, he spotted her in her shorts and halter-top sitting cross-legged in the middle of the dance floor surrounded by papers. He stole up behind her and kissed her on top of her head.

"Hi! What are you doing home already?"

"I sold our three prize Holstein bulls at the auction and got top dollar. So, I decided there was no point hanging around Calgary. Figured I might as well come home to see my beautiful wife." As Danny spoke his large calloused hands began to massage Kathy's bare back. "I'm assuming that Cindy is still playing in the basketball game after school?"

Kathy grinned as she leaned forward enjoying the massage. "That's right, Danny and Chrissy won't be coming over because she's in Cochrane playing the piano at the Seniors Centre. She'll pick up the girls after the basketball game. I told her and Joel to come for supper around about seven o'clock."

Danny grinned broadly. "It's a good thing that I picked up a keg of wine. It's such a rare occasion when we're alone for an afternoon. Whatever are we going to do with ourselves?"

Kathy smiled up at him and closed her eyes. He gave her a kiss then sat down and moved very close to her. "Oh, Danny, I would love to share our afternoon and the wine with you, but my parents are here standing right behind you."

Danny jumped to his feet and whirled around. Nate and Julia stood in the centre of the room grinning at him. "Nate and Julia, when did you arrive?"

"Why, Danny, we came and had lunch with Kathy. The reason that you didn't see our car is because Chrissy's car needs to be repaired so she borrowed ours to go into town. Our daughter wanted to sort through her papers to show us what she's found out about her past, or I should say how little she's found out. Julia and I were just finishing doing the lunch dishes when we heard somebody sneaking in the front door and got worried." Nate showed Danny the golf club that he had hidden behind his back to deal with any intruder. "I thought maybe your prize driver would come in handy."

Danny chuckled. Turning back to Kathy he asked, "Honey, are all these papers from your search?"

"Yes, they are. Danny, you know I've contacted government departments, the adoption registry; the Church of the Latter Day Saints, and even scanned years of obituaries and done land title searches in the archives. Well, these are all the papers I've collected. Mom and dad have told me all the details they know about my adoption, but I just can't find any evidence that indicates whether my birth mom is still alive or whether she died. Really all I know is that my birth parents were married to each other. Her name was Tessa and at some point she was in a terrible car accident. We know that her deceased husband, my birth father, was named Ethan and that he definitely died in the accident."

Kathy shook her head and then threw her hands up into the air. "I don't know. Maybe it's just hopeless to be trying to find someone with so little information."

Julia sat down at the piano bench and began to play quietly. Suddenly she stopped. "Kathy, I don't think that anything we've told you from our meeting with Mrs. Arkins was incorrect, but then again I think we're dealing with a cover-up. Your birth father's family is supposed to be very powerful and powerful families have connections with people in high places."

"I'm not really surprised that you haven't been able to find out anything, Kathy." Nate added, "Reputation is everything to those types. The records probably still exist, but were most likely ordered sealed away in a government vault. Only one way I can think of to solve this is by doing an end play to find your birth mom." Nate lowered his huge frame into the comfort of a leatherette lounge chair.

"What do you mean by an end play, Dad?"

"Well, why don't you copy Chrissy's example and use the power of the press? Advertise your search."

Danny shook his hand. "Nate, wouldn't that assume that the other person is also interested in reading those advertisements?"

"Yes, but you know, it's amazing how many people are interested in reading that section of the newspaper. A lot of people these days are looking to find lost loved ones and search out their roots. I would start in Alberta, then advertise in British Columbia and Saskatchewan. Make sure that you advertise in all the urban and the rural papers."

Julia smiled lovingly at Danny and Kathy then looked at Nate and nodded toward the door. "My goodness, will you look at the time! Kathy, it's time your dad and I started getting on home."

Kathy looked at Danny then at her parents. "Mom, for goodness sakes. You are not walking to Cochrane. I'm sure that Danny doesn't mind driving you home. Do you, honey?"

"Of course not. Let's go jump in the truck—I'll have the two of you home in five minutes flat."

"Kathy," Julia interjected, "I'll have you know that when Nate and I operated this ranch, we used to walk to town all the time. We're older, but I can still dance circles around you and Chrissy and your dad still gives Danny and Joel a fair day's labour. Now we're going to leave the two of you alone. Tell Chrissy to bring our car back when she has a chance."

Seconds later, Danny and Kathy stood watching as hand in hand Nate and Julia strode off down the section road toward Cochrane. Silently they closed the curtains and lit a solitary candle. They smiled lovingly at each other, poured a glass of wine and then turned out the lights.

* * *

A month later, Kathy and Danny had completed their advertisements in the British Columbia, Alberta and Saskatchewan newspapers. Not a phone call or written response had been received by Kathy until one day just as Cindy and Rochelle came bursting into the ranch house after school, the telephone rang and Cindy picked it up.

Kathy was still upstairs teaching their final student when Cindy called up the stairs, "Mom, there's a woman on the phone who wants to talk to you."

"Thanks, Cindy. I'll take the call up here."

Later, when Kathy came down the staircase to join Chrissy, their husbands, and children for coffee, Cindy asked, "Who was that on the phone, Mom? Somebody's mother I'll bet asking how their kid's doing, eh?"

Kathy stared at Cindy for a few seconds, then replied, "Yes, Cindy, you're right. It was a mother concerned about her child."

Chrissy, Danny, and Joel watched as Kathy poured herself a cup of coffee. Her hand was trembling and the coffee splattered on the counter. Slowly, Kathy put the pot of coffee back on the coffee maker. Putting a hand on her forehead, she stood looking out of the kitchen window.

Danny rose from his chair. Looking at the others, he said, "People, I could really use some help moving those heifers over to the north pasture. Joel, don't you have steers over at your place that you want moved as well?" Joel nodded his head and got up. "Okay everybody, go on ahead and saddle up our horses."

"Mom, aren't you coming? We haven't ridden together for quite a while." Cindy stood looking at Kathy.

Kathy never turned to look at Cindy, as she quietly whispered, "No, not this time Cindy."

"But Mom..."

"I think your mother is tired. Why don't we let her have a rest? Go on down to the sheds and help Rochelle saddle up the horses." Danny smiled at Cindy and gently pointed her toward the door.

As the others walked out of the kitchen, Chrissy paused and looked at Kathy then gently touched her shoulder. Chrissy kissed her friend on the cheek, then without saying a word turned and went outside to join the others.

Danny walked up behind Kathy and said,

"Tell me what is the matter, Kathy?"

Kathy's face was ashen-coloured as she slowly turned and stared up at her husband. "She's found me, Danny! Our advertisement worked. My birth mother is alive—that was her on the phone! Oh, Danny, suddenly I'm so scared." Danny wrapped his arms around her. "She's my birth mother, but she is a complete stranger to me. Next Monday she wants to meet us in Kelowna. Can you believe it? Both Chrissy and I finding our birth mothers and they both live in Kelowna!" Kathy continued to speak rapidly. "My mom taught me to love and be strong. To her dancing and singing are ways of helping us appreciate the beauty of everything around us. Dad taught me to successfully deal with problems in a factual, analytical fashion. I have all these skills my parents have given me, and I don't know what to say to the woman who gave birth to me."

"Honey, you are one of the strongest people I have ever known. Don't worry. Everything will turn out okay. After all, without you this ranch would not run so efficiently. Now, I'm going to phone your parents to see if they can take care of Cindy and then I'll phone to get us some airline reservations."

* * *

The following Monday, at seven o'clock in the morning, their flight from Calgary landed in Kelowna. Inside the busy terminal was a tall distinguished-looking gentleman dressed in a western suit, carrying a sign with Kathy and Danny Thompson printed on it in big bold letters.

Danny grasped Kathy's right hand firmly in his then stepped forward and extended his free hand. "Good morning. My name is Danny Thompson and this is my wife, Kathy."

The lean man took off his cowboy hat, bent his head slightly and then shook hands with the Thompsons. He looked at Kathy for a few long minutes, smiled, and then replied, "Kathy and Danny, it is an honour to meet both of you. I'm Doctor Cyrus Hewitt, but please just call me Cyrus. My wife, our six kids and their families thought it would be best if I picked you up rather than overwhelming you with around thirty of our clan. You'll get to meet the whole bunch out at the ranch later today. Of course, Kathy, that won't happen until you and your birth mom have had a private meeting." Cyrus's eyes twinkled as he observed the startled reaction on Kathy and Danny's faces. Anyway, my wife is waiting for you at the ranch. So, let's get in the land rover and get on our way."

Danny looked at Cyrus. "Cyrus, are you a rancher or a doctor?"

"I'm both. I love the ranch life, but I also find it rewarding to use my skill as a surgeon to help people. Also, we find it helps to pay the bills."

The three of them went out to the parking lot. Cyrus drove them to a Best Western Hotel near the Orchard Park Mall in Kelowna and waited for them while they freshened up.

Then they drove out to the ranch. As they were approaching the ranch house, Kathy was startled to see a tall, elegant woman dressed in jeans and a brightly decorated blouse walking toward them. She felt her heart start to pound. It was like looking into a mirror. Cyrus brought the vehicle to a lurching stop and jumped out to give the woman a kiss. Then he took his wife by her hand and pointed at Kathy who sat rigidly in the back of the vehicle. When Kathy turned, she found that Danny had opened her door and was extending his hand to her. As she got out Danny offered his arm to her, which she gratefully accepted. Grinning, Cyrus brought his wife forward.

"Tessa, this lovely lady has to be your twin because you sure don't look old enough for her to be your daughter."

Tessa smiled joyfully at Kathy as she said, "Oh, Cyrus, you old charmer." She reached out her arms to Kathy. "All those years I cried myself to sleep worrying about what had happened to her and here she is a grown beautiful woman." The two women hugged each other tightly. Finally, after stepping away from the embrace, Tessa murmured, "Cyrus, I can be completely at peace now, for my babies have survived that terrible time."

Danny studied Tessa and Cyrus for a few minutes. "Kathy and I really don't know what you are talking about."

Tessa smiled and said, "Cyrus, would you go into the house and get me the album that I made for Kathy?"

Cyrus left, then quickly returned with the album and gave it to his wife.

"Come on," he said to Danny, "let's leave the ladies alone for a bit. Come up to the house. Everybody is inside waiting. I'm sure Kathy will tell you everything when you are alone tonight. I'll introduce you to our kids, their spouses and the grandchildren. We've always sung when we want to celebrate and we find that music helps us through our troubles. So, don't be surprised if they want you to join in a sing song."

Danny looked at Cyrus with a bemused look on his face then laughed. "Cyrus, I'm kind of like you. I'm a structural engineer, and also a rancher. However, music is definitely not part of my talents. Kathy and our daughter, Cindy, are the musical ones in our family."

Tessa took Kathy by the arm. She carried the large album under her other arm. They walked up a high hill overlooking the azure-coloured Okanogan Lake. Sitting down on an old hardwood bench, Tessa turned toward Kathy. She placed her two hands on the sides of Kathy's face and stared into Kathy's eyes then put her hands in her lap as she started to talk. "Kathy, thirty-six years ago a man named Ethan Ashcroft and I met at the University of Calgary and fell in love. Phillip Ashcroft, Ethan's father, told his son that his family was against our romance and that Ethan was to terminate our relationship immediately, but we loved each other so much that we ignored their wishes. My dad was a postal worker and mom was a seamstress—positions that the Ashcrofts felt were not good enough for their esteemed social position. Our parents were all very bitter and refused to have anything to do with each other. We went against their wishes, left the university and were married secretly. We then moved out to a small country town named Dalemead. Our parents disinherited us so we kept to ourselves as much as possible.

Being in love, we went ahead and had our first baby. We sent birth announcements to our families, but sadly neither side ever acknowledged that they had a grandchild. Aunt Courtney Ashcroft, Phillip Ashcroft's sister, was the only Ashcroft that ever visited our little house at Dalemead. In the next year of our marriage our second beautiful blue-eyed daughter was born. We named the baby after Aunt Courtney. You were that baby, Kathy.

A month later while we were travelling on the Trans-Canada Highway to visit one of my friends in Vernon, a huge logging truck entered the road unsafely. We swerved to try and miss the truck, but we ended up going down a cliff near Revelstoke. Ethan was killed and I was so seriously injured that the doctor thought I might not survive and if I did, I'd never walk again. There was no one to look after my precious babies, so I signed the appropriate papers so that a loving family could adopt you. It was the saddest day of my life. I've always carried the memory of you and your sister in my heart and prayed that you were placed with loving families and that you were happy."

"My sister? I have a sister?"

"Yes. Both you and your sister were adopted."

Kathy sat absolutely still in stunned silence as Tessa continued her story. "Cyrus was the surgeon who operated on me. It was through his skill and determination that I not only survived, but also learned to walk again. Cyrus and I tried to find out where my babies had gone, but of course by that time it was too late—you had both been adopted."

Kathy sat looking up at the fruit trees in blossom. Finally she took a deep breath. "Tessa, you said that they took away your other baby—my sister. Do you know where my sister is?"

Tessa put her hand on Kathy's. "I'm coming to that part of the story, Kathy, but first here are some pictures that we took of you and your sister when you were just babies."

She handed the album to her, then walked away a few steps to give Kathy a few moments to herself.

Kathy laid the album on her lap and slowly opened it. The first few pages showed a baby in a crib and crawling on the floor. The next pages showed a child of about two years old and a baby And then the album pages were blank.

Quietly closing the book, tears in her eyes, Kathy whispered, "My sister. I never knew I had a sister. Do you know where she is?"

Tessa smiled. "This is part of the miracle. It was only a few months ago that your sister found me! She came out to the ranch and we had a wonderful reunion. Here, I've brought a picture of her and her husband to show you," added Tessa.

Reaching into her pocket, Tessa extracted the picture for Kathy and reverently handed it to her. Kathy stared in shock and disbelief as she found herself looking at a picture of Chrissy and Joel!

Tessa put an arm around Kathy as she continued on, "I hope you will get to know her and become good friends."

Kathy's mind was whirling as she attempted to grasp her newfound knowledge. She thought to herself, '*Chrissy! Chrissy who has always been there for me. I have always loved her like a sister. My friend is a part of me.*'

Tessa was watching Kathy intently, a puzzled look on her face. "Kathy…are you all right?"

Slowly Kathy took her wallet out of her purse. She extracted a picture of Chrissy and handed it to Tessa. A look of amazement crossed Tessa's face.

In a very soft voice Kathy began to speak. "Tessa, Chrissy has been my friend ever since we were in Elementary School together. She is the best girlfriend that a person could ever have had. She's always been there and like a sister to me!"

Tessa slowly sank down to sit beside Kathy. After a few moments she said, "I choose to believe that God has brought you and Chrissy together. I think that He wanted to ensure that you watch out for each other.

"Kathy, although I'm your mom, you have a mom and dad who love you. All I ask is that we be friends and keep in contact. I'd love to be part of your life now. And Chrissy's too."

Kathy smiled broadly as she looked into Tessa's eyes. "My dad, Nate Racine, said that I had to do an end play like Chrissy and use the power of the press to find you. Now, despite all the obstacles that were placed in front of you, Chrissy, and myself, we have come back together. We are kindred spirits and have found each other. Tessa, I would like to go back to the house now to rescue Danny, and to meet the rest of the family."

The two women stood up and walked arm in arm back down to the ranch house. Inside they could hear singing. When they entered the house, Kathy started to laugh as she saw Danny trying to play the bongo drums as Tessa's large family sang, '*I Saw the Light*.' Carrying her album Kathy walked over to sit beside her husband.

Laying aside the bongo drums, he whispered, "You all right, honey?"

Kathy looked up, her eyes shone, and a broad smile appeared on her face. "Danny, you won't believe what I learned. Chrissy is my sister!"

"You're kidding! Well, as I've always said, you two *are* just like sisters."

"I'll explain it all to you later at the hotel."

At that moment Tessa's family brought the song to an end. Tessa asked the whole family group to sit, and then she introduced Kathy to her new three half-sisters and three half-brothers.

The six siblings grinned at Kathy and then one of the sisters said, "Kathy, when we found out that the second lost sister had been found, we were just so happy for mom. The circle is completed now. We would like to welcome you to our family by each of us telling you a bit about our children and ourselves. We're also hoping that you and Danny will do the same, to help us get to know you. But first, a rather unusual and crazy sounding request— Danny tells us that you're a great dancer and singer! How about we girls entertain the others with a song? It's kind of a custom out here at the folk's place that we sing for our supper, Kathy. Are you interested?"

Kathy shook her head, grinned, and playfully punched Danny on the shoulder. "Danny has a big mouth, but yes, I would love to sing with my new sisters."

Kathy's soprano voice blended beautifully with Tessa and her sisters as they sang, '*On The Wings Of A Dove*.' After the song, Danny escorted Kathy over to an old leather lounge seat where they sat together with Danny's arm around her. Tessa smiled lovingly at her large family and motioned for quiet. She stood up beside the piano and accompanied by one of her daughters, sang a beautiful ballad that spoke of loved ones coming together. Cyrus then disrupted the concert by entering the room dressed in a barbecue apron and announcing that it was suppertime.

The next afternoon, Cyrus and Tessa drove Kathy and Danny to the airport. As the four of them stood at the Departures Gate waiting for the announcement for final boarding, Kathy looked at Cyrus and said, "Thank you for helping Tessa, Cyrus."

When the announcement came for Danny and Kathy's flight, Tessa opened her arms to Kathy who stepped forward to hug the woman who was forced to give her up so many years ago. Then she stepped back to hold Tessa's hands in hers. "I will phone you after I talk to Chrissy. We'll need to talk about getting together in the future."

"I'll be looking forward to our next get-together. I'm sure that Chrissy will be all right. Just tell her in the way that is most comfortable for you. Good luck!"

Danny shook hands with Tessa and Cyrus, and then walked with Kathy onto the tarmac and up the steps to the airplane. They turned and waved goodbye before disappearing inside.

* * *

As the sleek jet lifted off the runway, Danny's hand firmly grasped Kathy's. Gravely, Kathy looked upward for assurance into his gentle eyes and he smiled lovingly downward at her. Nestling her head into his broad shoulder, Kathy stared out of the window of the aircraft as they winged their way home to Calgary.

Chrissy, Joel, and the kids were there to pick them up.

"Well," asked Chrissy impatiently. "How'd

it go?"

Kathy gave a warning look that said, '*Remember Cindy doesn't know what's up yet?*' "It was a good trip," murmured Kathy. "We'll talk later." She bent to give Cindy a big hug.

"Come on," Joel said. "Let's go get the car and be on our way home."

Joel drove them back out to the country following Highway 2A to the hills behind Cochrane. Cindy kept trying to talk to her mother about how the trip was and what she had done. Kathy sat mutely staring out of the window. Every once in a while she would nervously glance at Chrissy, then would go back to staring at the scenery.

Danny leaned forward and put a hand gently on Cindy's shoulder. "Your mother is tired, Cindy. She needs a bit of quiet time."

"But I just want to hear about your trip! Nobody even told me why you were going to Kelowna. It's not fair, Dad. How come I can't know?"

Danny put an arm around Cindy and smiled at her. "Not now, sweetheart, later."

Kathy, worrying about how she was going to break the news to Chrissy, was hardly aware of the talking around her. The thought ran through her mind that she shouldn't be afraid, but she was. She loved Chrissy, and didn't want anything to jeopardize their friendship.

Danny whispered into Kathy's ear, "Darling, just tell Chrissy. Don't prolong this situation. She is your best friend. She'll understand."

"Danny, I can't. Please let me do it in my own way," Kathy whispered back.

Joel turned off of the highway and drove along the section road that led to Kathy and Danny's home. When they entered the darkened house, Kathy walked on ahead of the others and climbed the stairs to her dance studio. Then she sat down at her favourite dormer window seat to stare out at the darkened countryside. Behind her she heard footsteps enter the loft and turned to look. Danny stood there quietly looking at her with Cindy leaning back against him.

"Kathy, are you okay?"

"Yes."

"What are you doing?"

"Just thinking."

"Do you want me to put the coffee on? Chrissy, Joel, and Rochelle are sitting down at the table waiting for us."

"Danny, I need to tell Chrissy what's happened."

Cindy marched across the dance floor and over to her mom, her face determined. "Mom, will somebody please tell me what happened in Kelowna and what the heck is happening now? What is all the big mystery?"

Kathy held out her arms to her daughter. "I'm sorry, Cindy."

"Mom, you scare me when you act all mysterious and secretive. I'm fourteen years old now and I think I should be included in solving whatever it is. I mean, I'm your daughter, Mom, and...your always telling me how smart I am. Aren't I smart enough and old enough to be included?" Cindy nestled back into her mother's arms.

Smoothing back Cindy's beautiful hair, Kathy kissed her on the end of her nose. "I'm sorry, sweetheart. It's just that I find it hard to talk about some things."

Danny smiled at her and nodded his head.

Kathy continued hesitantly, "Sweetheart…I went to Kelowna to meet my birth mother."

"Cool, Mom! How was it?"

"It was wonderful. She is a lovely lady who has six grown children and sixteen grandchildren."

"What's her name?"

"My birth mother's name is Tessa Hewitt. She lives on a ranch just outside of Kelowna with her husband Doctor Cyrus Hewitt."

Cindy suddenly moved out of her mother's arms. Pacing back and forth between her parents she shook her head. "Dad and Mom, do you know what this means?"

"No, what does it mean?" Danny said with a big smile as he sat down beside Kathy.

Cindy stopped her pacing then turned to stare first at Danny and then at Kathy. "Well, for one thing, it means that dad and I have to get busy putting all our new relatives on our computerized Christmas list. Number two, it means that I have a new grandma, grandpa, aunts, uncles, and cousins to get to know. Number three, I would just like to know where are they all going to sleep when they come to visit us. And…" Cindy stopped when she saw that Kathy's hand was held up in the stop position.

Kathy stood up, walked over to Cindy, and took her two hands. "Sweetheart, I know you have lot of questions and I have a lot of things to tell you, but right now I need to talk to Chrissy."

"Let's go down and tell her the story together."

Danny walked over to Cindy, put his hands gently on her shoulders, and said, "Your mom needs to tell Chrissy something very important, and to do that she needs for us to leave them alone."

Cindy shook her head. "Now you're keeping things from me again!"

Danny and Kathy looked over Cindy's head into each other's eyes.

Kathy's voice became a whisper as she slowly spoke.

"Cindy, come over here by the window." Kathy and Danny walked over to her favourite window seat and sat down. Cindy sat between them, waiting, with a troubled look on her face. "Sweetheart, when I met my birth mother she shared with me that I had a sister who was also adopted. She showed me a picture of my sister and Cindy...Chrissy is my sister."

"Are you kidding, Mom?"

"No, sweetheart, it's true."

"Cool, Mom! Let's go tell her the great news!"

"No, Cindy. This is something special that I have to do by myself. I want you to promise me that you won't say a word to Chrissy, Joel, and Rochelle until I have told her. Okay, sweetheart?" Kathy looked down into Cindy's eyes. Cindy gravely nodded her head up and down, then suddenly a great big angelic grin spread across her face. She leaped to her feet and began pacing back and forth between her mom and dad.

"Mom, this *is* cool! It means Rochelle's mom is my Aunt Chrissy! And Rochelle is my cousin!"

"Danny, would you take Cindy with you and send Chrissy up to see me, please? I guess I'd better find a way to tell her."

"Honey, just tell her. Chrissy has been your friend ever since elementary school. She'll be okay with the news."

"I hope so. Would you take Joel and the girls outside for a walk and send Chrissy up here?"

"I'd be glad to, Kathy. Come on, Cindy, let's go."

Danny took Cindy by the hand and they walked downstairs together. A few minutes later, Kathy, watching from the dormer window, saw Joel and Danny walking down the road with the two girls. Danny turned to give her the thumbs up signal. Kathy then pulled the curtains of the dance studio. She heard Chrissy starting slowly up the stairs, and she raced over to a stack of CDs to find a very special selection.

When Chrissy entered the studio, a puzzled look on her face, Kathy was sitting with her back against the wall. She looked up at her friend and smiled. "Hi, Chrissy!"

Sitting down beside Kathy, Chrissy took her hand in hers. "Hi, yourself! All right, Kathy, it's time to tell me what's going on. You hardly said a word to anyone on the way in from the airport."

Kathy slowly uncrossed her long legs and stood up. She smiled lovingly down at Chrissy. "Chrissy, I want to dance and sing for you."

Chrissy laughed. "Okay. Do you want me to play the piano for you, Kathy?"

"No, Chrissy. Could you just put this CD in the machine, please?"

"Sure."

The music began and at first Kathy just danced as Chrissy sat quietly, listened and watched. Kathy paused in her dancing and took Chrissy's hands in hers, then began to sing the song:

The Kindred Spirits

I have a friend who is my kindred spirit.
I've always thought that she's like a sister to me.
My loved ones fulfill and strengthen me in so many different ways.
Sometimes though, I have wished that I had a sister,
Because sisters share with each other in a special way,
But my friend has been that sister that I never had.
She has always been there for me.
I am so happy that I could cry because now I know,
That she is oh so much more than a best friend,

For she is the sister that I thought I never had.

As Chrissy looked into Kathy's eyes her heart began to race and she said, "You danced and sang beautifully. Does that song mean what I think it does?"

"Yes."

"Kathy, are you trying to tell me something? Oh, Kathy, something unexpected happened in Kelowna didn't it? I think I know what you are trying to tell me...but I'm almost afraid to believe that it's true."

Kathy walked away from Chrissy and pulled a tissue out of her pocket to dab her eyes. Then she turned, opened the curtains and stared out of the window. Chrissy slowly walked up behind Kathy and put an arm around her longtime friend's shoulder. Placing a hand over Chrissy's, Kathy continued to gaze out of the window. In the distance, she could see Danny and the others playfully chasing each other.

"Chrissy, we truly *are* sisters. Tessa showed me the picture she'd taken of you and Joel when you visited her ranch last year."

Chrissy slowly turned Kathy around and looked into her eyes. "Oh Kathy, I think for the first time in my life I am absolutely speechless!"

Both women hugged tightly, tears streaming down their faces.

As Danny and Joel looked up toward the window, both smiled broadly and gave the thumbs up signal to each other.

Don M. McKay was born and raised in Calgary, Alberta. He attended the University of Calgary where he received his Master of Arts degree. Don worked as an educator for thirty years. He is married and has two grown children. *Josephine Remembers And Other Stories* is the author's second collection of short stories. The author's first book is titled, *Josephine And Other Canadian Short Stories.*

To Order Additional Copies Of

JOSEPHINE REMEMBERS

AND OTHER STORIES

CONTACT

BLACK HAT PUBLISHING
5208 44 AVE. NW
CALGARY, ALBERTA
CANADA
T3A 0L8

Phone: (403) 288 5734
E-Mail: Skeena@TelusPlanet.net